Jean sire de Joinville, James Hutton

Saint Louis - King of France

Jean sire de Joinville, James Hutton

Saint Louis - King of France

ISBN/EAN: 9783337336011

Printed in Europe, USA, Canada, Australia, Japan

Cover: Foto ©Andreas Hilbeck / pixelio.de

More available books at **www.hansebooks.com**

SAINT LOUIS, KING OF FRANCE.

BY THE SIRE DE JOINVILLE.

TRANSLATED BY JAMES HUTTON

Third Edition.

LONDON:
SAMPSON LOW, SON, AND MARSTON,
CROWN BUILDINGS, 188, FLEET STREET.
1870

NOTICE.

THIS translation of the Sire de Joinville's "History of Saint Louis" is a literal rendering into English of the French edition published by Messrs. Daunou and Naudet in their "Recueil des Historiens des Gaules et de la France," tome XXième. For the arbitrary division of the work into chapters the translator alone is answerable. The first book has also been considerably abridged, in order to avoid tedious repetitions; the same incidents being related at greater length in the course of the subsequent narrative.

CONTENTS.

Chapter V.

Chapter VI.

Chapter VII.

Chapter VIII.

Chapter IX.

Chapter XIV.

Chapter XV.

SAINT LOUIS, KING OF FRANCE.

CHAPTER I.

TO his good Lord Louis, son of the King of France, by the grace of God King of Navarre, Count Palatine of Champagne and Brie,[1] John, Sire de Joinville, his Seneschal of Champagne, Greeting. Love, Honour, Right Willing Service.

Dear Sire, I make known to you that Madam the Queen, your mother, who loved me much (to whom God be merciful!) entreated me as earnestly as she could that I would cause a book to be written of the holy words and good deeds of our sainted King Louis. I made her that promise, and by God's help the book is finished, in two parts.

The first part relates how St. Louis ruled himself throughout his whole life, according to God and the Church, and for the good of his realm.

---

[1] Louis X, surnamed Le Hutin, son of Philip the Fair, was King of Navarre and Count of Champagne and Brie, by right of his mother, Jane of Navarre.

The second part of the book speaks of his great chivalry and great deeds of arms.

Sire, because it is written: "Do first what belongs unto God, and He will direct all thy other works," I have caused to be written what pertains to the three things above-named ; that is to say, what pertains to the profit of soul and of body, and what pertains to the government of the people.

For these other matters, I have had them written also to the honour of that true saint, because by these things above-named it will be clearly seen that never did a layman of our times live so devoutly during the whole of his days, from the commencement of his reign down to the very end of his life. At the end of his life I was not myself present ; but Count Peter of Alençon, his son, was there, who loved me much, and described to me the fine end he made, and which you will find written out in the latter part of this book. And thereupon it seems to me that enough has not been done for him, seeing that he has not been placed in the army of martyrs, notwithstanding the great pains he endured in the pilgrimage of the cross for the space of six years that I was in his company, and that he imitated our Lord even to the cross. For if God died on the cross, so did he ; for he wore the cross when he was at Tunis.

The second book will speak of his great chivalry and great hardihood, which were such that I saw him four times place his own body in peril of death, as you shall hear in the right place, in order to save his people from hurt.

Now I say unto you, Monseigneur, King of Navarre, that I promised Madam the Queen, your mother, (to whom God be merciful !) that I would make this book ; and to acquit myself of my promise, I have made it.

And because I see no one who ought to have it so rightly as yourself, who are his heir, I send it to you that you and your brothers, and others who shall hear it read, may take good example from it, and put these examples into practice, that God may be pleased with them.

In the name of Almighty God, I, John, Sire de Joinville, Seneschal of Champagne, cause to be written the life of our sainted Louis, what I saw and heard for the space of six years that I was in his company in the pilgrimage over the sea, and since we returned from it. And before I recount to you his great exploits and feats of arms, I will tell you what I saw and heard of his holy words and sage teachings, that they may be found in their order for the edification of those who shall hear them. This holy man loved God with all his heart, and imitated His works; which appeared in this that, as God died for the love He had for His people, he also several times imperilled his life for the love he had for his people, when he could have done otherwise had he wished, as you will hear by-and-bye. The love he had for his people was shown in what he said to his eldest son during a sore sickness which he had at Fontainebleau.

" Fair son," said he, " I pray you make yourself beloved by the people of your kingdom ; for, truly, I would rather that a Scotsman should come from Scotland and govern the people justly and loyally, than that you should govern badly in the sight of all."

The saint loved truth to such a degree, that even with the Saracens he would not draw back from what he had promised them, as you will hear by-and-bye. As to his palate, he was so indifferent, that never in my life did I hear him ask for any particular dish, as many rich men do, but he eat contentedly of what his cooks served up to him. He was measured in his speech, for never in my life did

I hear him speak ill of any one, nor did I ever hear him name the devil, a name widely spread through the realm, which cannot, I think, be pleasing to God. He diluted his wine by measure, according as he saw the wine would bear it. He asked me in Cyprus why I put no water into my wine; and I answered him the reason was because the physicians had told me that I had a large head and a cold stomach, and therefore need not fear becoming intoxicated. He replied that they deceived me, for if I did not learn in my youth to dilute my wine, and wished to do it in my old age, I should be attacked with gout and pains of the stomach, so that I should never have health; and if in my old age I drank wine by itself, I should become intoxicated every evening, and it was a sorry thing for a man of worth to get drunk.

He asked me if I wished to be honoured in this world and enter Paradise through death. I answered, yes; and he said to me, " Keep yourself, then, from doing or saying anything wittingly which if all the world knew you could not avow it, and say, ' I did this, I said that.'"

He told me to refrain from contradicting or gainsaying anything that was said in my presence, provided there would be no sin or hurt in my remaining silent, because hard words engender strifes which have cost the lives of thousands.

He used to say that a man ought so to dress and equip his person, that the greybeards of the day should not be able to say that it was overdone, nor the young men, that there was something wanting. This was recalled to my mind by the father of the king who now reigns,[1] in alluding to the embroidered coats-of-arms which are fashioned nowadays. I made answer to him that never,

---

[1] Philip the Hardy, father of Philip the Fair.

in the voyage over the sea I made, did I see embroidered coats-of-arms, either on the king, or on anyone else. And he told me that he had coats embroidered with his arms which had cost him 800 livres parisis. I replied that he would have made a better use of them had he bestowed them for the love of God, and had made his coats of good taffety (*cendal*), ornamented with his arms, as his father used to do.

The sainted king was at Corbeil one Whitsuntide, with eighty knights in his company. After dinner, the king went down into the meadow below the chapel, and spoke at the gateway to the Count of Brittany, the father of the present duke, whom God preserve! Master Robert de Sorbon came in quest of me, and taking hold of the end of my mantle, led me to the king, and all the other knights came after us.

Then I asked Master Robert, "Master Robert, what do you want with me?"

And he said to me, "If the king were to sit down in this meadow, and you were to seat yourself on a bench above him, I wish to ask you if you would be worthy of blame?"

I answered him, yes.

He continued: "Then you do a thing much to be blamed, seeing that you are more magnificently dressed than the king; for you attire yourself in furs of different colours and in green cloth, which the king does not do."

I made him answer: "Master Robert, with your permission, I do nothing to be blamed if I clothe myself in furs of different colours and in green cloth, for it is the dress left me by my father and my mother. On the contrary, it is you who are to blame, for you are the son of a *villain* father and a *villain* mother, and you have abandoned the dress of your father and your mother, and

clothe yourself in richer camlet than the king." Then
I took the flap of his surcoat and that of the king's surcoat, and said, " See, now, if I speak the truth."

Whereupon the king undertook, with all his might, to
defend Master Robert.

Some short time afterwards, my lord the king summoned Monseigneur Philip, the father of the present king,
and King Thibaud, and sat down at the door of his
oratory, and, placing his hand on the ground, said :—

" Sit down here, quite close to me, so that no one
may hear us."

"Ah, sire," replied they, "we dare not sit so close to you."
Then he said to me, " Seneschal, sit down here."

I did so, and so close to him that my robe touched his.
And he made them sit down next to me, and said to them :

" You did very wrong, you my sons, in not doing at
once what I commanded you ; take care that does not
happen again."

And they said they would never again do so.

Then he said to me that he had called us to him that
he might confess to me that he was wrong in defending
Master Robert against me.

" But," he added, " I saw he was so taken aback, that he
much needed help from me. For all that, do not you
regard what I may have said in defence of Master
Robert ; for, as the seneschal asserted, you ought to
dress well and becomingly, because your wives will love
you the more, and your people will value you the more.
For, as the sage remarks, we ought so to adorn ourselves
in apparel and armour that the greybeards of this age
shall not be able to say that we have done too much, nor
the young men of this age that we have not done
enough."

He told me that Bishop William of Paris had related to him how that a great master in theology once came to him and said that he wished to speak to him. The bishop replied :—

" Master, say whatever you wish to say." And when the master was about to speak to the bishop, he began to weep very bitterly ; so the bishop said to him : " Master, speak. Do not be down-hearted, for no one can sin so much that God cannot forgive yet more."

" I tell you, sir," said the master, "that I cannot but weep; for I look upon myself as an infidel, because I cannot bring my heart to believe in the sacrament of the altar, as it is taught by the holy Church, and yet I know right well that it is one of the temptations of the enemy."

" Master," said the bishop, "tell me, when the enemy sends you this temptation, is it pleasing to you?"

To which the master made answer :—

" Sir, on the contrary, it annoys me as much as anything can annoy me."

" Now, I ask you," continued the bishop, "would you accept gold or silver on condition that you should utter with your lips something against the sacrament of the altar, or against the other holy sacraments of the Church?"

" I, sir!" exclaimed the master. " Know that there is nothing in the world that I would accept on that condition. I would rather that they tore all my limbs out of my body than say anything of the kind."

" I will now say something else to you," the bishop observed. " You are aware that the King of France is at war with the King of England; and you are also aware that the castle which is nearest to the frontier between the two is La Rochelle, in Poitou. I will therefore ask you one question: if the king had entrusted you with the custody of La Rochelle, which is on the frontier, and had consigned to me the keeping of the castle of Laon, which is in the heart of France, and in a land at peace, to whom ought the king to be most grateful at the end of his war—to you, who had guarded La Rochelle without losing it, or to me, who had guarded Laon ?"

"In heaven's name, sir," cried the master, "it would be to me, who had guarded La Rochelle without losing it."

"Master," resumed the bishop, "I tell you that my heart is like the castle of Laon, for I have no temptation or doubt touching the sacrament of the altar. Wherefore I say to you that for once God is pleased with me because I believe steadfastly and in peace, He is pleased four times with you, because you keep your heart for Him in the war of tribulation, and have such goodwill towards Him that for no earthly good, nor for any hurt that could be done to your body, would you forsake Him. I tell you, therefore, to be quite at your ease, for that your state under these circumstances is more pleasing to our Lord than my own."

When the master heard that, he knelt down before the bishop, and was well content.

The sainted king recounted to me how certain persons from among the Albigenses went to the Count de Montfort, who at that time was holding their country for the king, and said to him that they had come to see the body of our Lord, which had become flesh and blood in the hands of the priest. And he said to them :—

"Go and see it, you who do not believe in it. For my part, I believe firmly all that the holy Church tells us about the sacrament of the altar. And do you know," added the count, "what I shall gain by believing in this mortal life all that the holy Church teaches us? I shall have a crown in the heavens rather than the angels who behold Him face to face—for which reason they cannot help believing in Him."

He related to me how there had been a great conference of clergy and Jews at the monastery of Cluny. There was a knight there to whom the abbot had given food for the love of God, and he asked the abbot to let him have the first word, a request that was granted with some reluctance. Then he stood up, and resting upon his crutches, asked that they would cause the greatest clerk and greatest rabbi of the Jews to come to him; and they did so. And he asked the following question:

"Master," said the knight, "I ask you if you believe that the Virgin Mary, who carried God in her womb and in her arms, was a virgin and yet mother of God."

And the Jew replied that of all that he believed nothing at all. Then the knight answered that truly he had acted like a madman in entering her church and her house, when he neither believed in her nor loved her.

"And verily," added the knight, "you shall pay for it."

Thereupon he lifted up his crutch and struck the Jew on the ear, and knocked him down. The Jews then took to flight, and carried off their wounded rabbi, and that was the end of the conference. Then the abbot went up to the knight and told him that he had committed a great folly. But the knight replied that the abbot had been guilty of a greater folly in summoning such a conference; for before the conference would have been brought to an end there were a great many Christians there who would have gone away unbelievers because they would not have properly understood the Jews.

"Therefore, I tell you," said the king, "that no one, if he is not a very clever clerk, ought to dispute with them; but a layman, when he hears the Christian law evil spoken of, should not defend that law save only with his sword, which he ought to run into the infidel's belly as far as it will go."

57. — The king governed his land rightly and loyally, and according to God, as you will learn hereafter. He had his work regulated in such a manner, that Monseigneur de Nesle, and the good Count de Soissons, and the rest of us who were about his person, after attending mass, went to hear the pleadings at the gateway, now called the Court of Requests; and when he returned from church he sent for us, and seating himself at the foot of his bed, he made us sit down around him, and asked us if there were any cases to dispose of which could not be disposed of without him. We mentioned such to him, and he commanded that they should be brought before him, and asked them: "Why do you not take what my people offer you?" And they would say: "Sire, it is because they offer too little." Then he would answer them: "You would do well to take what they wish you to take." Thus the holy man exerted himself with all his might to put them in the path of justice and reason.

Many a time it happened that in summer time he would go and sit down in the wood at Vincennes, with his back to an oak, and make us take our seats around him. And all those who had complaints to make came to him without hindrance from ushers or other folk. Then he asked them with his own lips: "Is there any one here who has a cause?" Those who had a cause stood up, when he would say to them: "Silence all, and you shall be despatched one after the other." Then he would call Monseigneur de Fontaines or Monseigneur Geoffroy de Villette, and would say to one of

them: "Dispose of this case for me." When he saw
anything to amend in the words of those who spoke for
others, he would correct it with his own lips. Sometimes in summer I have seen him, in order to administer
justice to the people, come into the garden of Paris
dressed in a camlet coat, a surcoat of woollen stuff
(*tyreteinnes*), without sleeves, a mantle of black taffety
(*cendal*) round his neck, his hair well combed and without coif, a hat with white peacock's feathers on his head.
Carpets were spread for us to sit down upon around
him, and all the people who had business to despatch
stood about in front of him. Then he would have it
despatched in the same manner as I have already described in the wood of Vincennes.

The king's loyalty was shown in the affair of Mon- 66,
seigneur de Trie, who brought to the holy man a charter which affirmed that the king had conferred upon the
heirs of the Countess of Boulogne, the last who died,
the county of Dammartin, in Gouelle. The seal of the
charter was broken, so that there only remained one
half of the legs of the king's figure on the seal, and the
stool on which his feet rested. He showed it to all of us
who were of his council, and said that we must help him
with our advice. We all of us answered, without any
one dissenting, that he was in no way bound to execute the
charter. Then he told John Sarrazin, his chamberlain,
to hand him the letter which he had asked of him.
And when he had got the letter he said to us: " Sirs,
this is the seal which I used before I went across the
sea, and you may see clearly from this that the impres-
sion on the broken seal is similar to the seal that is
entire. Therefore, I dare not with a clear conscience
hold back the said county." Then he called for Monseigneur de Trie, and said to him, " I make over the
county to you."

CHAPTER II.

N the name of Almighty God we have thus far written a portion of the good words and pious teachings of our sainted King Louis, in order that those who shall hear them may find them in their proper order, so that those who hear them may better profit by them than if they had been written amongst the following deeds.   And now we shall begin to speak of his actions, in God's name and in his own.

As I have heard him say, he was born on the day of St. Mark the Evangelist, shortly after Easter.[1] On that day the cross is carried in procession in many places, and in France they are called black crosses.   It was therefore a sort of prophecy of the great numbers of people who perished in those two crusades; to wit, in that of Egypt, and in that other, in the course of which he died at Carthage; for many great sorrows were there on that account in this world, and many great joys are there now in Paradise on the part of those who in those two pilgrimages died true crusaders.

[1] April 25th, A. D. 1215.

He was crowned on the first Sunday in Advent.[1] The mass for that Sunday begins in this wise: "*Ad te levavi animam meam.*" And what follows is this: "Fair Sire God, I will lift up my soul unto Thee, I put my trust in Thee." He had perfect confidence in God even to his death, for, at the moment of dying, in his last words, he invoked God and His saints, and especially Monseigneur St. James and Madame Ste Geneviève.

God, in whom he put his trust, preserved him ever from his infancy to the very last; and specially in his infancy did He preserve him when he stood in need of help, as you will presently hear. As for his soul, God preserved it through the pious instructions of his mother, who taught him to believe in God, and to love Him, and placed about him none but ministers of religion. And she made him, while he was yet a child, attend to all his prayers, and listen to the sermons on saints' days. He remembered that his mother used sometimes to tell him that she would rather he were dead than that he should commit a deadly sin.

Sore need had he in his youth of God's help, for his mother, who came out of Spain, had neither relations nor friends in all the realm of France. And because the barons of France saw that the king was an infant, and the queen, his mother, a foreigner, they made the Count of Boulogne, the king's uncle, their chief, and looked up to him as their lord. After the king was crowned, some of the barons asked of the queen to bestow upon them large domains, and because she would do nothing of the kind, all the barons assembled at Corbeil. And the sainted king related to me how

---

[1] A. D. 1226.

neither he nor his mother, who were at Montlhéri, dared to return to Paris, until the citizens of Paris came, with arms in their hands, to fetch them. He told me, too, that from Montlhéri to Paris the road was filled with people with or without weapons, and that all cried unto our Lord to give him a long and happy life, and to defend and preserve him from his enemies. And God did so, as you will presently learn.

At the parliament held by the barons at Corbeil, those who were present agreed among themselves, as it is said, that the good knight, Count Peter of Brittany, should rebel against the king. They also agreed that they would in person obey the summons the king would issue against the count, and that each should take with him only two knights. They did this to see if the Count of Brittany could vanquish the queen, who was a foreigner, as you have already heard. And many persons say that the count would have vanquished the queen and the king, if, in this hour of need, the king had not had the aid of God, who never failed him. The aid which God gave him was such that Count Thibaud of Champagne, who was afterwards King of Navarre, came to help the king with 300 knights, and because of the support the count rendered to the king, the Count of Brittany was obliged to submit himself to the king's mercy. The upshot of all this was that, to make peace, he had to leave in the king's hands the counties of Anjou and Le Perche.

After the king had vanquished Count Peter of Brittany, all the barons of France were so enraged against Count Thibaud of Champagne, that they resolved to send for the Queen of Cyprus, who was the daughter of the eldest son of Champagne, to disinherit Thibaud, who was a son of the second son of Champagne. Some

among them undertook to reconcile Count Peter with
Count Thibaud, and the affair was arranged in such a
manner, that Count Thibaud promised to take to wife
the daughter of Count Peter of Brittany. The day
was fixed on which the Count of Champagne was to
espouse the damsel, who was to be brought to him for
espousals to an abbey in Prémontré, near Château-
Thierry, called, I think, Val-Secret. The barons of
France, who were nearly all related to Count Peter,
took the trouble to conduct the damsel to Val-Secret,
to be espoused, and gave notice of their arrival to the
Count of Champagne, who was at Château-Thierry.
But while the Count of Champagne was on his way to
marry her, Monseigneur Geoffroy de la Chapelle came
to him from the king with a letter of credence, and
said to him : " Sir Count of Champagne, the king has
heard that you have made an agreement with Count
Peter of Brittany to marry his daughter. The king
therefore enjoins you, if you would not lose all you
possess within the realm of France, not to do so, for
you know that the Count of Brittany has done worse
to the king than any man living." The Count of Champagne, upon the advice of those who were with him,
then returned to Château-Thierry.

When Count Peter and the barons of France, who
were waiting at Val-Secret, were informed of this, they
were all furious at the slight he had passed upon them,
and straightway sent to fetch the Queen of Cyprus.
And as soon as she had come, they engaged themselves
to one another to summons all the men-at-arms they
could raise, and to invade Brie and Champagne from
the side of France, and that the Duke of Burgundy,
whose wife was the daughter of Count Robert of Dreux,
should enter the county of Champagne from the side

of Burgundy, with a view to take the city of Troyes, if possible. The duke called together all the people he could, and the barons did likewise. Then the barons came burning and ravaging from one side, and the Duke of Burgundy from another; and the King of France, on his part, hastened to oppose them. So sore was the trouble of the Count of Champagne, that he himself fired his towns before the barons could come up, that they might not find them habitable. Besides other towns which he burned, the Count of Champagne set fire to Epernay, Vertus, and Sezanne.

The burghers of Troyes, when they saw that they had lost the succour of their lord, sent to Simon, Seigneur de Joinville, the father of the present Seigneur de Joinville, to come and help them. And he, having called together all his men-at-arms, set out from Joinville by night, as soon as the tidings reached him, and arrived at Troyes before it was day. Thereby the barons were foiled in the plan they had laid for taking the said city, and, consequently, passed on from before Troyes, and went and pitched their tents in the meadow, near to where the Duke of Burgundy was.

The King of France, who knew that they were there, marched straight thither to give them battle; and the barons sent to him, and entreated him, so far as he was personally concerned, to retire to the rear, while they gave battle to the Count of Champagne, the Duke of Lorraine, and the rest of the king's followers, with 300 knights less than had the count and duke. But the king answered them that they should not do battle with his people unless he was with them in person. So they returned to him and said, that if such was his pleasure, they would gladly bring the Queen of Cyprus round to peace. The king replied that he would not listen to anything about peace, nor suffer the Count de Champagne to do so, until they had evacuated the county of Champagne. And they evacuated it in such sort, that from Isles, where they were, they went and encamped beneath Juilly; and the king pitched his tents at Isles, whence he had driven them. And when they knew that the king was there, they went on to Chavence, but dared not await the king, and so moved on to Laignes, which belonged to the Count of Nevers, who was of their party. In this manner the king reconciled the Count of Champagne and the Queen of Cyprus, and peace was concluded on these conditions, that the said Count of Champagne should give to the Queen of Cyprus land to the value of about 2000 *livres* a year, and 40,000 *livres* down, which the king paid for the count. And the Count of Champagne sold to the king, in consideration of these 40,000 *livres*, the following fiefs; to wit, the fiefs of the counties of Blois, Chartres, Sancerre, and the viscounty of Châteaudun. It was said by some that the king only held these fiefs in pledge; but that is not the case, for I put the question to our sainted King Louis beyond sea.

Let us now return to our matter, and tell how, after these events, the king held a great court at Saumur in Anjou. I was there myself, and I testify to you that it was the best managed one I have ever seen, for at the king's table there sat next to him the Count of Poitiers, whom he had knighted on the feast of St. John, and next to the Count of Poitiers sat Count John of Dreux, whom also he had recently knighted; after the Count of Dreux came the Count of La Marche; after the Count of La Marche, the good Count Peter of Brittany. And in front of the king's table, facing the Count of Dreux, sat Monseigneur the King of Navarre,

c

in coat and mantle of *samit*,[1] handsomely ornamented with a girdle, a clasp, and a cap of gold, and I carved before him. In front of the king, his brother, the Count of Artois, waited upon him, and the good Count John of Soissons carved the meat. To guard the table there were Monseigneur Imbert de Beaujeu, who was afterwards constable of France, and Monseigneur Enguerrand de Coucy, and Monseigneur Archambault de Bourbon. Behind these three barons there were fully thirty of their knights in coats of cloth and silk, to guard them; and behind these knights there stood a great number of sergeants clad in the livery of the Count of Poitiers, wrought upon taffety (*cendal*). The king was dressed in a coat of blue samit, and a surcoat and mantle of scarlet samit lined with ermine, and upon the head a cotton cap which became him badly, because he was then a young man. The king held this banquet in the market-halls of Saumur, and the people said that the great King Henry II. of England had built them expressly for giving such great banquets. His market-halls are built in the style of the cloisters of the Cistercian monks, but I suspect that there are no cloisters so long as these. And I will tell you why I say so, for against the wall of the cloisters in which the king sat at meat, and was surrounded by knights and sergeants who took up much space, there dined at one table twenty bishops or archbishops; and again, after the bishops and archbishops, there dined close to that table the Queen Blanche, his mother, at the end of the cloister on the opposite side to where the king was seated. And to serve the queen, there were the Count of Boulogne, who was afterwards King

---

[1] Cloth of silver or gold manufactured at Venice.

of Portugal, and the good Count of St. Pol, and a German eighteen years of age, said to be the son of St. Elizabeth of Thuringia, for which reason Queen Blanche used to kiss him on the forehead from a feeling of reverence, because she thought his mother must have kissed him there many a time.

At the other end of the cloister were the kitchens, butleries, pantries, and offices; from this cloister were brought the meat, wine, and bread which were served up before the king and queen. And in all the other aisles, and in the open space in the middle, there dined such a number of knights that I could not count them; and many persons said that they had never seen so many surcoats and other vestments of cloth of gold at any banquet as there were there: it was reported that there were quite 3000 knights.

After this festival the king conducted the Count of Poitiers to Poitiers to receive the homage of his vassals; but when the king arrived there he would have been very glad to have been back in Paris, for he found that the Count of La Marche, who had eaten at his table on St. John's day, had collected as many men-at-arms as he could at Lusignan, near Poitiers. The king was detained nearly a fortnight at Poitiers, and dared not depart until he had come to terms with the count. More than once I saw the Count of La Marche come from Lusignan to speak with the king at Poitiers; and each time he brought with him the Queen Dowager of England, his wife, mother of the King of England.[1] And many asserted that the king and the Count of

---

[1] Isabella of Angoulême, widow of King John, and mother of Henry III.

Poitiers patched up a bad peace with the Count of La Marche.

After the king had returned from Poitiers, no long time elapsed before the King of England came into Gascony to make war against the King of France. Our sainted king, with all the force he could gather together, took horse to give him battle. Then the King of England and the Count of La Marche came before a castle called Taillebourg, situated upon a dangerous river named the Charente, which cannot be crossed there except over a very narrow stone bridge. As soon as the king reached Taillebourg, and the armies came in sight of each other, our people, who had the castle on their side, made great exertions, and with much peril crossed over in boats and by bridges, and rushed upon the English. When the king beheld that he put himself in the same danger as the others, for, for one man the king had when he crossed over to the English side, the English had a hundred. For all that it came to pass, as it pleased God, that when the English saw the king cross over, they lost heart, and retreated into the city of Saintes, and many of our people, entering with them pell-mell, were made prisoners.

Those of our side who were taken reported that a great dispute arose between the King of England and the Count of La Marche, and the king declared that the count had sent for him and said that he would find great help in France. That same evening the King of England departed from Saintes, and returned into Gascony.

The Count of La Marche, like a man who had no help for it, surrendered himself a prisoner to the king, and brought with him his wife and children. By reason of that, in making peace with the count, the king received a good deal of land, but how much I know not, for I was not present at that affair, because I had not yet put on the hauberk.[1]   But I have heard it said that, together with the land, the king gained 10,000 *livres parisis,* which the count previously received from the king's treasury every year.

While we were at Poitiers, I saw a knight named Monseigneur Geoffrey de Rancon, who, for some great outrage done him by the Count of La Marche, had sworn upon holy relics that he would never have his hair cut after the knightly fashion, but would wear it long, and parted down the middle, as women do, until he had seen himself avenged on the count, either by himself or by others.   And when Monseigneur Geoffrey saw the Count of la Marche, with his wife and children, kneeling before the king, and begging for mercy, he caused a bench to be brought, and had his hair cut close in the presence of the king, the count, and the others who were there.   In this expedition against the King of England and his barons, the king, as I have been told, bestowed costly gifts upon those who survived it.   But neither for the gifts nor the expenses occasioned by this expedition, or by others on this or on the other side of the sea, did the king ever require or take any aid to be complained of from his barons or knights, from his vassals or trusty towns.   Nor was there any marvel in this, for he acted upon the advice of his good mother, who was with him, and to whose counsels he conformed, and upon that of the discreet men who remained to him from the times of his father and grandfather.

---

[1] That is, was not yet one-and-twenty.

CHAPTER III.

A. D. 1243.

FTER these things it chanced, as it pleased God, that great illness fell upon the king at Paris, by which he was brought to such extremity that one of the ladies who watched by his side wanted to draw the sheet over his face, saying that he was dead; but another lady, who was on the other side of the bed, would not suffer it, for the soul, she said, had not yet left the body. While he was listening to the dispute between these two ladies, our Lord wrought upon him and quickly sent him health; for before that he was dumb, and could not speak. He demanded that the cross should be given to him, and it was done. When the queen his mother heard that he had recovered his speech, she exhibited as much joy as could be; but when she was told by himself that he had taken the cross, she displayed as much grief as if she had seen him dead.

After the king put on the cross, Robert, Count of Artois, Alphonse, Count of Poitiers, Charles, Count of Anjou, who was afterwards King of Sicily, all three brothers of the king, also took the cross, as likewise did

Hugh, Duke of Burgundy, William, Count of Flanders, brother to Count Guy, of Flanders, the last who died, the good Hugh, Count of Saint Pol, and Monseigneur Walter, his nephew, who bore himself right manfully beyond sea, and would have been of great worth had he lived. There were also the Count of La Marche, and Monseigneur Hugh le Brun, his son; the Count of Sarrebourg, and Monseigneur d'Apremont, his brother, in whose company I myself, John, Seigneur de Joinville, crossed the sea in a ship we chartered, because we were cousins; and we crossed over in all twenty knights, nine of whom followed the Count of Sarrebourg, and nine were with me.

At Easter-tide, in the year of grace 1248, I summoned my vassals and retainers to Joinville, and on the Easter-eve, when all my people whom I had summoned had come, was born John, my son, Sire d'Ancarville, by my first wife, who was sister to the Count of Grandpré. We had feasting and dancing all that week, in the course of which my brother the Sire de Vaucouleurs and other rich persons who were there gave banquets one after the other on Monday, Tuesday, Wednesday, and Thursday.

I said to them on the Friday : "Sirs, I am going away beyond sea, and know not if I shall ever return ; so draw near to me. If I have done you any wrong I will redress it, one after the other, as is my practice with all who have anything to ask of me or my people." I made amends to them according to the decisions of those dwelling on my lands ; and, that I might not influence them, I withdrew from their deliberations, and carried out without dispute whatever they decided.

Because I was unwilling to take away with me any money that did not belong to me, I went to Metz, in

Lorraine, to mortgage a large tract of my lands. And on the day that I left our country to go to the Holy Land I was not worth a thousand livres a year in land; for my lady-mother was still living. And yet I went with nine knights, and was one of three knights bannerets. I mention all this because if God—who has never failed me—had not been my help, I could hardly have borne up against it for so long as the six years I spent in the Holy Land.

Just as I was preparing to set out, John, Sire d'Apremont and Count of Sarrebourg by right of his wife, sent to me and informed me that he had arranged his affairs to go beyond sea with nine knights, and that if I were willing we could charter a vessel between us. To this I agreed, and his people and mine hired a ship at Marseilles.

The king summoned his barons to Paris, and made them swear to keep faith and loyalty towards his children if anything happened to himself on the voyage. He asked the same of me, but I refused to take any oath, because I was not his vassal. While I was on the way I encountered in a cart three dead men whom a clerk had slain, and whom they were taking to the king. When I heard that, I sent one of my squires with them to know how it had happened; and the squire whom I sent related to me how the king, when he came out from the chapel, went out to the doorsteps to see the dead bodies, and asked the Provost of Paris how it had happened. And the provost told him that the dead men were three of his sergeants of the Châtelet, who went upon the by-roads to rob people.

" They met," said he to the king, "the clerk whom you see here, and stripped him of all his clothes. The clerk ran away in his shirt to where he lodged and fetched his

crossbow, and gave his hunting-knife to a boy to carry.
When he came up with them, he called to them and
told them that they should die. The clerk then presented his crossbow, discharged it, and pierced one to
the heart. The two others took to flight, but the clerk,
snatching the hunting-knife from the boy, pursued after
them by the light of the moon, which was then bright
and clear. One of them thought to get through a hedge
into a garden, but the clerk struck at him with the
knife," continued the provost, " and cut through one leg
so that it only hung on by the skin, as you see here. The
clerk then took up his chase after the other, who tried
to get into a neighbouring house where the people were
still up; but the clerk struck him with the knife on the
top of the head so stoutly that he clove him to the teeth,
as you may see here," said the provost to the king.
" Sire," he went on, " the clerk told what he had done
to the provost nearest to his street, and then came and
placed himself in your prison. So I bring him to you,
Sire, to do with him according to your pleasure : here
he is."

"Sir clerk," answered the king, " you have missed
being a priest through your prowess ; and because of
your prowess I take you into my service, and you shall
go with me beyond sea. And this engagement I give to
you because I desire that my servants should see that
I will not support them in any of their misdoings."

When the people who were collected there heard
these words, they cheered our lord, and prayed that
God would grant him a long and happy life, and would
bring him back in triumph and in health.

After all this I went back to our own country, and the
Count of Sarrebourg and myself agreed to send our
armour in carts to Auxonne, to embark it there on the

river Saône to be conveyed to the Rhône. The day that I left Joinville I sent for the Abbot of Cheminon, who was considered the worthiest man of the order of White Monks. I had heard strong testimony in his favour once at Clairvaux, at the festival of Our Lady, when our sainted king was there, given by a monk who pointed him out to me and asked if I knew him. I said to him: "Why do you ask me?" And he replied: "Because I look upon him as the worthiest man in the whole order of White Monks. I will tell you, too, what I heard related by a discreet man who was in bed in the same sleeping apartment as the Abbot of Cheminon. The abbot had uncovered his chest because of the heat; and this worthy man, who was abed in the chamber in which the abbot was asleep, saw the Mother of God go up to the abbot's bedside and draw her robe over his chest for fear the draught might do him a mischief."

This Abbot of Cheminon gave me my scarf and pilgrim's staff, and then I set out from Joinville, without ever again entering the castle until my return on foot, without shoon, and in my shirt; and I went in this fashion to Blécourt and St. Urban, and to other holy places that are there. And while I was on the road to Blécourt and St. Urban I took care never to turn my eyes towards Joinville, lest my heart should soften over the pleasant château I was leaving and my two children.

My companions and myself dined at Fontaine-l'Archevêque, before Dongeux, where Abbot Adam of St. Urban (whom may God absolve) bestowed many jewels upon myself and upon the knights who were with me. Thence we went to Auxonne, where we embarked with our armour on board boats to descend the Saône as far as Lyons; and by the side of the boats were led our warhorses.

At Lyons we embarked on the Rhône to go to Arles-le-Blanc; and upon the Rhône we passed a castle called Roche de Gluy, which the king had destroyed because Roger, the lord of the castle, was accused of despoiling merchants and pilgrims.

In the month of August we went on board our ships at the Rock of Marseilles. The day we embarked the door of the vessel was opened, and the horses were led inside that we were to take with us; then they fastened the door and closed it up tightly, as when one sinks a cask, because when the ship is at sea the whole of the door is under water. When the horses were in, our sailing-master called out to his mariners who were at the prow : " Are you all ready ?" And they replied : " Sir, let the clerks and priests come forward." As soon as they had come nigh, he shouted to them: " Chant, in God's name !" And they with one voice chanted: " *Veni, creator Spiritus.*" Then the master cried to his men: " Set sail, in God's name !" And they did so. And in a little time the wind struck the sails and carried us out of sight of land, so that we saw nothing but sea and sky; and every day the wind bore us farther away from the land where we were born. And thereby I show you how foolhardy he must be who would venture to put himself in such peril with other people's property in his possession, or while in deadly sin ; for when you fall asleep at night you know not but that ere the morning you may be at the bottom of the sea.

At sea a wonderful adventure happened to us, for we sighted a mountain that was quite round, over against the coast of Barbary. We sighted it about the hour of vespers, and sailed all night, and fancied we had made over fifty leagues, and yet on the morrow we found ourselves still opposite the very same mountain ; and so it happened to us twice or thrice. When the mariners saw that, they were sore dismayed, and told us that our ships were in great peril, for we were opposite the land of the Saracens of Barbary. Thereupon a worthy priest, who was called the Dean of Maurupt, said to us that he had never suffered in his parish from drought, or from too much rain, or from any other scourge, but that, as soon as he had made three processions on three Saturdays, God and His Mother delivered him. It happened to be a Saturday; we made the first procession round the two masts of the ship; for myself, I was carried on men's arms, because I was grievously sick. After that we saw no more of the mountain, and on the third Saturday reached Cyprus.

When we reached Cyprus the king was already there, and we found an immense supply of stores for the king; to wit, the king's wine-stores and granaries. The king's wine-stores consisted of great piles of casks of wine, which his people had purchased two years before the king's arrival, and placed in an open field near the seashore. They had piled them one upon the other, so that when seen from the front they looked like a farmhouse. The wheat and barley had been heaped up in the middle of the fields, and at first sight looked like hills; for the rain which had long beaten upon the corn had caused it to sprout, so that nothing was·seen but green herbage. And when it was desired to convey it into Egypt, they broke off the outer coating with the green herbage, when the wheat and barley within were found as fresh as if they had only just been threshed out.

The king, as I have heard him say, would gladly have pushed on to Egypt without stopping, had not his barons advised him to wait for his army, which had not all arrived.

While the king was sojourning in Cyprus, the great Cham of Tartary sent envoys to him, the bearers of very courteous messages. Among other things, he told him that he was ready to aid him in conquering the Holy Land and in delivering Jerusalem out of the hands of the Saracens. The king received the messengers very graciously, and sent some to him, who were two years absent before they could return to him. And with his messengers the king sent to the Cham of Tartary a tent fashioned like a chapel, which cost a large sum of money, for it was made of fine rich scarlet cloth. And the king, in the hope of drawing them to our faith, caused to be embroidered inside the chapel, pictures representing the Annunciation of Our Lady, and other articles of faith. And he sent these things to them by the hands of two friars, who spoke the Saracen language, to teach and point out to them what they ought to believe. The two friars came back to the king at the time his two brothers were returning to France, and found the king, who had departed from Acre where his brothers had left him, at Cæsarea, which he was fortifying, and where there was neither peace nor truce with the Saracens. How the envoys of the King of France were received I will tell you, as they themselves related it to the king; and in the report they made to the king you will hear much that is strange, but which I will not recount just now, because I should be obliged to interrupt the narrative I have already commenced, and which I now resume.

I, who had only a thousand livres a year from land, had taken upon myself when I went beyond sea to maintain nine knights and two knights-bannerets. It came to pass, therefore, that when I reached Cyprus, there remained to me only 240 *livres tournois*, after paying for my ship. On this account some of my knights warned

me that if I did not provide myself with money, they
would leave me. But God, who has never failed me,
brought it about so that the king, who was at Nicosia,
sent for me and took me into his own service, and placed
800 livres in my coffers; after that I had more money
than I wanted.

During the time we abode in Cyprus, the Empress of
Constantinople sent me word that she had arrived at
Paphos, a city of Cyprus, and that I and Monseigneur
Erard de Brienne were to go and fetch her. When we
came there we found that a violent wind had snapt the
anchor ropes of the ship, and driven her to Acre, and
that there remained to her of all her baggage nothing but
the mantle she was wrapped in and a dinner robe. We
conducted her to Limisso, where the king and queen and
all the barons welcomed her with all honour. On the
morrow I sent her cloth to make a dress, and taffety
(*cendal*) to line it with. Monseigneur Philip de Nanteuil, the trusty knight, who was in attendance upon the
king, met my squire on his way to the empress. When
the worthy man saw that, he went to the king and said
that he took great shame to himself, and to the other
barons, that no one had thought before of sending any
clothing to the empress. The empress came to ask
succour from the king for her lord, who had remained at
Constantinople, and she managed so well that she carried
off with her a hundred letters and more from myself and
other friends she had there; in which letters we bound
ourselves by oath that, if the king or the legate would send
300 knights to Constantinople after the king himself had
set out for home, we would go there. And to fulfil my
oath, at the moment we were about to return, I prayed
the king, in the presence of the Count of Eu, whose
letter I have, to send thither 300 knights, of whom I

would be one. But the king replied that he had not the means, and that, however well filled his treasury might have been, he had emptied it to the last coin. After we had arrived in Egypt, the empress went away into France, and took with her Monseigneur John of Acre, her brother, whom she married to the Countess of Montfort.

At the time of our coming to Cyprus, the Sultan of Iconium was the richest king in all the land of the paynims, and he had done a wonderful thing, for he had melted down a large portion of his gold into earthen pots, which he caused to be broken, so that the lumps of gold remained exposed to view in one of his castles, and any one entering the castle could both see and touch them: there were six or seven of them. His great wealth was shown in a tent which the King of Armenia sent to the King of France, and was worth quite 500 livres; and the King of Armenia informed him that it had been given to him by a *ferrais* of the Sultan of Iconium. Now a *ferrais* is the officer who takes care of the sultan's tents and sweeps out his palaces.

The King of Armenia, to free himself from the yoke of the Sultan of Iconium, went to the Cham of Tartary and did homage to him in order to have his aid, and obtained from him such a multitude of men-at-arms that he was able to give battle to the Sultan of Iconium. The battle lasted a long time, and the Tartars killed so many of the sultan's men, that nothing had since been heard of him. Because of the great rumour that prevailed in Cyprus of the battle which was to take place, some of our sergeants passed over into Armenia to be present at and to assist in winning the victory, but not one of them ever came back to us.

The Sultan of Babylon (Cairo), who expected that the

king would arrive in Egypt in the spring-time, conceived the design of overthrowing the Sultan of Emessa, who was his enemy, and accordingly went to besiege him in his city of Emessa. The Sultan of Emessa was in no condition to contend with the Sultan of Babylon, and saw clearly enough that if he lived long enough he would overthrow him. He therefore worked upon the sultan's *ferrais* to such purpose, that the latter poisoned his master. The poisoning was in this wise. The *ferrais* bethought him that the sultan went every day after dinner to play at chess upon the mats which were at the foot of his bed; so he poisoned the mat upon which he knew the sultan sat every day. It happened thus, that the sultan, who was barefooted, turned himself upon an excoriation he had on one of his legs. Immediately the poison entered the quick and deprived him of all movement of one half of his body on the left side. For two days he neither eat, nor drank, nor spoke. His people left the Sultan of Emessa in peace, and carried back their master into Egypt.

CHAPTER IV.

S soon as March came round, the king, and, by his command, the barons and other pilgrims, gave orders that the ships should be laden with wine and provisions, to be ready to sail when the king gave the signal. Thus it happened that when everything was ready the king and queen withdrew on board their ship on the Friday before Whitsunday (A. D. 1249), and the king desired his barons to follow after in his wake straight towards Egypt. On the Saturday the king set sail, and all the other vessels at the same time, which was a fine sight to behold, for it seemed as if the whole sea, as far as the eye could reach, was covered with sails, and the number of ships, great and small, was reckoned at 1800. The king cast anchor at the end of a promontory called the Point of Limisso, and all the other vessels around him. The king went on shore on Whitsunday. When we had heard mass, a strong and violent wind blowing from Egypt rose so high that of 2800 knights whom the king was taking with him into Egypt, there were not more than 700 whom the gale did not separate from the king's company and drive to Acre and other foreign lands, and who did not rejoin him until long afterwards.

D

On the day after Pentecost the wind fell. The king and the rest of us who had remained with him, as it pleased God, set sail afresh, and fell in with the Prince of Morea and the Duke of Burgundy, the latter having bided awhile in the Morea. On the following Thursday the king arrived before Damietta, and we found there all the sultan's forces on the sea-shore; fine troops to look at, for the sultan's arms are of gold, and the sun striking upon the gold made the arms shine forth brilliantly. The noise they made with their cymbals and Saracenic horns was frightful to hear.

The king summoned his barons to take counsel as to what he should do. Many advised him to wait until his people had come up, because he had with him not one-third of his army; but he would not listen to them, and the reason he gave was that he should thereby inspire his enemies with courage, especially as near Damietta there was no port where he could wait for his people, so that it was to be feared that a mighty wind might take us and drive us to other lands, as had happened to our comrades on the day of Pentecost.

It was resolved that the king should land on the Friday before Trinity Sunday, and give battle to the Saracens, if they did not decline it. The king commanded Monseigneur John de Beaumont to lend a galley to Monseigneur Erard de Brienne and myself, in order to take ourselves and our knights ashore, because the large ships could not come near enough to the land. As God willed it, on my return to my ship I found a small vessel which Madame de Baruth, who was cousin-german to the Count of Montbéliard and myself, had given me, with eight of my horses on board. When Friday came, Monseigneur Erard and myself, in full armour, went to the king to ask for the galley; whereupon Monseigneur John de Beaumont told us we should not have it.

When our people perceived that we were not to have
the galley, they let themselves down out of the great
ship into the long-boat, as best they could.   When the
mariners saw that the long-boat was getting deeper and
deeper into the water, they escaped into the great ship
and left my knights in the boat.   Then I asked the
master how many there were in excess, and I also asked
him if he would take us safely ashore, if I put out a
certain number; and he answered, "Yes."   So I un-
loaded it in such a manner, that in three trips he brought
them to the vessel where my horses were.   While I was
taking our people across, a knight belonging to Monseigneur Erard de Brienne, named Plonquet, thought to
get out of the big ship into the boat, but the boat pushed
off, and he fell into the sea and was drowned.

When I returned to my ship, I put into my boat a
squire whom I knighted, and whose name was Monseigneur Hugh de Vaucouleurs, and two right valiant
bachelors, one of whom was Monseigneur Villain de
Versey, and the other Monseigneur William de Dammartin, who bore each other great enmity; and no one
could prevail upon them to make peace with one another,
because they had pulled each other by the hair in the
Morea.   But I made them forgive one another and
embrace each other, because I swore to them upon relics
that we would not land with them while hating each other.
Then we prepared to land, and came alongside the long- -
boat of the king's great ship, in which was the king
himself, whose people shouted after me because we were
going faster than they did, telling me to land beside the
oriflamme of St. Denis, which was borne on another
vessel that preceded the king's.   But I did not listen to
them.   On the contrary, I landed in front of a strong
body of Turks, where there were some 6000 men on

horseback.   As soon as they saw us upon the land, they spurred down upon us.   When we saw them coming we drove the points of our shields and the shafts of our spears into the sand, with the points towards them.   As soon as they saw that our spears would be into them, they faced about and rode off.

Monseigneur Baldwin de Reims, a worthy man, who had landed, sent word to me by his squire to wait for him, and I answered that I would do so with pleasure, for such a worthy man as he was might well be waited for in an hour of need; for which he bore me goodwill all his lifetime.   With him there came to us a thousand knights, and you must know that when I landed I had not a squire, or knight, or varlet with me of those I brought from my own country, and yet for all that God did not fail to aid me.

On our left hand landed the Count of Jaffa, who was cousin-german of the Count of Montbéliard, and of the Joinville lineage.   It was he who landed in the most noble style; for his galley was emblazoned within and without with his escutcheons, his arms being a cross *patée gules* on a field *or*.   He had fully 300 rowers in his galley, and every rower had a buckler with his arms, and on every buckler there was a pennon with his arms embroidered in gold.   As they came along, it seemed as if the galley flew, for the rowers plied their oars with all their might.   It seemed, too, as if a thunderbolt were falling from the skies, at the noise made by the pennons, and cymbals, and drums, and Saracenic horns that were in the galley.   As soon as the galley was driven as high up the strand as it could be, he and his knights leaped from the galley well-armed and well-appointed, and came and drew up by our side.

I had forgotten to mention that when the Count of

Jaffa had landed, he caused his tents to be pitched, and
when the Saracens beheld that they gathered together
in our front and again came spurring down upon us; but
when they saw that we did not give ground, they
wheeled round and galloped off.

On our right hand, at the distance of a good bow-
shot, the galley came ashore in which was the banner of
St. Denis. And there was a Saracen who, as soon as
they were landed, dashed into the midst of them, either
because he could not hold in his horse, or because he
fancied that the others would follow him, but he was cut
to pieces.

When the king heard that the oriflamme of St. Denis
had been borne ashore, he strode hastily along his ship,
and in spite of the legate who was with him and never
left him, he leaped into the sea, where the water came up
to his armpits. On he went, with his shield round his
neck, his helmet on his head, and lance in hand, until he
came up with his people who were on the shore. When
he got to the land and perceived the Saracens, he asked
what manner of men they were, and when he was told
that they were Saracens he clapped his lance under his
arm, threw his shield before him, and would have rushed
upon them, had the discreet men who were with him
suffered him to do so.

The Saracens three times sent word to the sultan by
means of carrier-pigeons that the king had landed, without receiving from him any instructions, because the
sultan was sick unto death; and when they saw that,
they believed that he was actually dead, and so evacuated Damietta. The king despatched a knight thither
to ascertain the fact, and the knight returned to the
king and said that he had been in the sultan's houses,
and that it was so. Then the king sent for the legate

and all the prelates with the army, and they chanted with loud voices : *Te Deum laudamus*. After that the king mounted on horseback, and all of us did the same, and went and pitched our tents before Damietta. It was a great oversight on the part of the Turks to leave Damietta without breaking up the bridge of boats, which would have embarrassed us sorely. But they wrought us much mischief at their departure by setting fire to the bazaar, where all kinds of merchandise were exposed for sale, and all things that are sold by weight. The consequence was as if some one to-morrow (from which God preserve us) were to set fire to the Petit-Pont at Paris.

We may well say, then, that Almighty God showed us great favour when he preserved us from death and from the perils of disembarkation, seeing that we landed on foot and attacked enemies who were on horseback. The Lord also showed us great favour in delivering Damietta into our hands, which we could not otherwise have taken without starving it into submission ; and that we can see clearly enough, because it was by famine that King John (of Jerusalem) took it (A. D. 1219) in the time of our fathers.

Our Lord can say of us as he said of the children of Israel : *Et pro nihilo habuerunt terram desirabilem*. And what did He go on to say ? He said that they forgat God who had saved them. And I will tell you by-and-bye how we too forgat Him. First of all I will speak to you of the king, who summoned his barons, clerks, and laymen, and required of them to help him in deciding how he should divide the spoils of the town. The patriarch was the first to speak. He said :—

" Sire, it seems to me that you should keep the wheat, barley, and rice, and all that is good for food, in order

to provision the town; and that it should be proclaimed through the camp that all other effects should
be carried to the legate's house, under pain of excommunication."

This advice was approved of by all the barons; but it
chanced that all the effects which were taken to the
legate's house did not amount to 6000 livres.

When this was done, the king and the barons sent for
Monseigneur John de Valery, a good man and true, and
spoke to him thus :—

"Sir de Valery," said the king, "we have agreed that
the legate shall hand over to you the 6000 livres to distribute as you think best."

"Sire," answered the worthy man, "you do me much
honour, for which I heartily thank you ; but the honour
and the offer you make me I must decline, please God,
for otherwise I should break through the good customs
of the Holy Land, which are that when the enemy's
cities are taken, of the spoils which are found therein
the king shall have one-third and the pilgrims the other
two-thirds. And this custom King John upheld when
he took Damietta, and, as our elders tell us, the kings
of Jerusalem who were before John also held to that
custom. So, if it please you to hand over to me the two-
thirds of the wheat, barley, rice, and other provisions,
I will gladly undertake to divide them among the
pilgrims."

The king refused to do so, and there the affair ended;
wherefore many persons were dissatisfied that the king
broke through the good old customs.

The king's people, whose duty it was to attract merchants by courteous treatment, let to them as dearly as
possible the shops where they were to sell their wares ;
and the report thereof went abroad through foreign

lands, and many merchants therefore gave up their intention of coming to the camp. The barons, who ought to have kept their money for the right time and place, began to give grand banquets with much ostentation. The common people took to bad women, whence it followed that the king dismissed a great many of his retainers when we returned from captivity. I asked him why he did so, when he told me that he knew for certain that within an easy stone's throw from his own tent brothels were kept by those whom he had dismissed, and that at the time of the greatest misery to which the army was ever reduced.

Let us now return to our subject and tell how, shortly after we had taken Damietta, all the sultan's chivalry came before the camp and besieged it on the land side. The king and all his chivalry armed themselves. I went in full armour to speak to the king, and found him also armed at all points and in the saddle, and with him several worthy knights who belonged to his own " battle." I asked permission for myself and my people to proceed forth from the camp to prevent the Saracens from hurling themselves into the midst of our tents. When Monseigneur John de Beaumont heard my request, he shouted aloud to me, and forbade me in the king's name to leave my tent until the king commanded me to do so.

I made mention just now of the worthy knights who were with the king, because he had with him eight, all good knights, who had performed gallant deeds of arms on both sides the sea, and such knights were usually styled *bons chevaliers*. The names of the knights who were attached to the king's person were—Monseigneur Geoffrey de Sargines, Monseigneur Matthew de Marly, Monseigneur Philip de Nanteuil, Monseigneur Imbert de Beaujeu, Constable of France, who was not there, but outside the camp with the master of the cross-bow-men and the greater part of the king's sergeants-at-arms, to guard the camp from any damage the Turks might strive to do unto it.

Then it came to pass that Monseigneur Walter d'Antrèche armed himself in his tent at all points, and when he had mounted his horse, his shield suspended from his neck, and helm on head, he ordered the flaps of his tent to be raised, and spurred towards the Turks; and at the moment he started from his tent, all alone, his followers shouted, "Chatillon!" But it chanced that before he reached the Turks he fell, and his charger passed over his body and galloped on, caparisoned with his arms, to the enemy, because most of the Saracens were mounted on mares, wherefore the horse was drawn towards them. And those who witnessed it told how four Turks came up to Seigneur Walter, as he was lying on the ground, and, in passing him, struck him heavy blows with their maces. Then the constable of France, with some of the king's sergeants-at-arms rescued him, and carried him in their arms to his tent. When he came there he was speechless. Several of the camp surgeons and physicians went to him, and because it seemed to them that there was no danger of death, they bled him in both arms. At a late hour of the evening, Monseigneur Aubert de Nancy proposed to me that we should go and see him, as we had not yet done so, and he was a man of great renown and valour. As we entered his tent, his chamberlain came up to us, and begged us to walk softly for fear of awakening his master. We found him lying on a coverlid of miniver, and, as we approached his bed very softly, we saw that he was dead. When this was told to the king, he replied that he should not like to have a thousand such, because they would be wanting to act without waiting for his commands, as this one had done.

The Saracens entered the camp every night on foot, and slew people wherever they found them asleep, whence it happened that they killed the sentinel of the Seigneur de Courtenay, and left him lying upon a table, but cut off his head, and carried it away with them, and this they did because the sultan gave a gold bezant for every head of a Christian. This annoyance was effected because the different battalions guarded the camp, each in its turn, on horseback; and when the Saracens wanted to enter the camp, they waited until the noise of the horses and men had passed on, then they entered the camp behind the horses, and issued from it again before it was daylight. The king, therefore, gave orders that the battalions which had been wont to go the rounds on horseback should do so on foot, so that the whole camp was placed in surety by our people who were on guard, because they were spread out so as to touch one another.

When that was arranged the king resolved not to leave Damietta until his brother, the Count of Poitiers, had arrived, who was bringing the last levies (*arrière-ban*) from France. And to prevent the Saracens from dashing into the camp on horseback, the king enclosed it with deep ditches, and every evening the cross-bowmen and sergeants kept watch and ward along these ditches, and also at the entrances to the camp. When St. Remy's day had passed (October 1st), without any tidings of the Count of Poitiers (about whom the king and the whole army were in great trouble, for they feared some misfortune had overtaken him), I related to the legate how the Dean of Maurupt had

caused us to make, at sea, three processions on three
following Saturdays, and how, before the third Saturday, we had landed at Cyprus.   The legate believed in
my story, and proclaimed, throughout the camp, three
processions for three Saturdays.   The first procession
sat out from the legate's house, and proceeded to the
church of Notre Dame, in the town, the said church
having been constructed in the Saracens' mosque, and
dedicated by the legate to the honour of the Mother
of God.   The legate preached a sermon on two
Saturdays when the king and the principal men of the
army were present, upon whom he bestowed plenary
indulgence.

Before the third Saturday, the Count of Poitiers
arrived, and it was well that he had not come sooner,
for in the space between the three Saturdays there had
been such a terrible tempest at sea before Damietta,
that fully 240 vessels, great and small, had been wrecked
and cast away, and the people on board drowned and
lost.   So that, had the Count of Poitiers arrived sooner
than he did, he and all his people would have been
swallowed up.

Upon the arrival of the Count of Poitiers the king
summoned all the barons of the army to decide in what
direction he should march, whether towards Alexandria,
or towards Babylon (Cairo).   Whence it resulted that
the good Count Peter of Brittany, and most of the
barons of the army, were of opinion that the king
should lay siege to Alexandria, because there is there a
good port where the vessels could lie that bring provisions for the army.   To this the Count of Artois was
opposed, and said that he could not advise going anywhere except to Babylon, because that was the chief
town in all the realm of Egypt; and he added, that

whoso wanted to kill a serpent outright should crush
his head. The king set aside the advice of his barons,
and held to that of his brother.

At the beginning of Advent the king set out with
his army to march against Babylon, as the Count of
Artois had counselled him. Not far from Damietta
we came upon a stream of water which issued from
the great river, and it was resolved that the army
should halt for a day to dam up this branch, so that it
might be crossed. The thing was done easily enough,
for the arm was dammed up close to the great river.
At the passage of this stream the sultan sent 500 of his
knights, the best mounted in his whole army, to harass
the king's troops, and retard our march.

On St. Nicholas' day (December 6th), the king gave
the order to set out, and forbade that anyone should be
so bold as to sally out upon the Saracens who were before us. So it chanced that when the army was in
motion to resume the march, and the Turks saw that
no one would sally out against them, and learned from
their spies that the king had forbidden it, they became
emboldened, and attacked the Templars, who formed
the advanced-guard. And one of the Turks hurled to
the ground one of the knights of the Temple, right
before the feet of the horse of brother Reginald de
Bichiers, who was at that time Marshal of the Temple.
When he saw that, he shouted to the other brethren:
" Have at them, in God's name ! I cannot suffer any
more of this." He dashed in his spurs, and all the
army did likewise. Our people's horses were fresh,
while those of the Turks were already done up.
Whence it happened, as I have heard, that not one of
them escaped, but all perished, several of them having
plunged into the river, where they were drowned.

CHAPTER V.

BEFORE going further, we must speak of the river which comes out of Egypt and the terrestrial Paradise; and I describe this for the better understanding of certain things that belong to my history. This river is different from all others, for, the further other rivers flow, the greater is the number of streams and rivulets that fall into them, but not one falls into this river; on the contrary, it happens that it comes, by a single channel, into Egypt, where it throws out its branches which spread themselves over the country. After St. Remy's day has passed, the seven branches flow over the land and cover the plains, and when the waters retire, the peasants go forth and till each his own piece of ground with a plough without wheels, with which they turn the soil over the wheat, barley, cumin, and rice, and this answers so well, that it cannot be improved. Nobody knows whence comes this swelling of the river, except it be by the will of God, and if it did not happen, nothing would come up in this country, because of the great heat of the sun, which would burn up everything, for it never rains there. The river is always turbid, so that the people of the country who wish to drink of it, take water from it in the evening, and crush into it four almonds or four beans, and on the morrow it is as good to drink as any one could wish. Before the river enters into Egypt, certain people, whose practice it is, spread out their nets in it in the evening, and in the morning they find in their nets objects of merchandise, which they sell by weight, and which are brought hither; to wit, ginger, rhubarb, aloes, and cinnamon. And it is said that these things come from the earthly Paradise; that the wind blows down the trees which grow in Paradise, just as it blows down the dead wood in the forests of this country; and the dead wood that falls into the river the merchants sell to us. The water of the river is of such a nature, that when we suspended it from our tent-ropes in the white earthenware vessels which they make in that country, it became in the heat of the day as cold as spring water. They told us that the Sultan of Babylon had many a time tried to find out where the river came from, and had sent people who carried with them a kind of bread called biscuit, because it is twice baked; and they lived upon this bread until they came back to the sultan. And they reported that they had ascended the river until they came to a huge precipitous rock, up which no one could climb. The river fell from the top of this rock, and it seemed to them as if there were a great quantity of trees upon the mountain above; and they said that they encountered strange wild beasts of different kinds, lions, serpents, elephants, that came and looked at them from the top of the river's bank, as they ascended the stream.

Let us now return to our subject, and describe how the river, after entering into Egypt, divides into branches, as I have already mentioned. One of these branches goes to Damietta, another to Alexandria, a third to Tanis, a fourth to Rexi. It was to this last branch that the King of France came with his army, and encamped between it and the Damietta branch. And all the sultan's forces were encamped upon the Rexi river on the opposite bank, facing our army, to prevent our passage, which was an easy thing to do, for no one could cross the river except by swimming.

The king resolved to make an embankment across the river to pass over to the Saracens. To protect those who were working at the embankment, the king caused two towers to be constructed, called cats' castles, for there were two castles in front of the "Cats,"[1] and two houses at the back of the castles to protect those who had to watch against the assaults of the Saracens' engines, for they had sixteen of them fully equipped. When we came there the king had eighteen engines made, over which Jocelyn de Cornant was master engineer. Our engines fired against theirs, and theirs against ours, but I never heard that ours did much damage. The king's brothers mounted guard by day, and we other knights by night, close to the "Cats." We arrived at the week before Christmas.

As soon as the "Cats" were finished the embankment was commenced, for the king was anxious that the Saracens, who fired at us without any cover across the river, should not wound those who had to carry the earth. As concerns this causeway the king and all the barons of the army acted like blind men; for, because they had dammed one arm of the river (which was easily done, because they took in hand to dam it up where it branched off from the main stream), they fancied they

---

[1] Covered galleries.

could also dam the Rixi arm, which was separated half a league from the main stream. To hinder the causeway which the king was constructing, the Saracens made holes in the ground on their side; and as soon as the river reached the holes it rushed into them and made a great ditch, whence it followed that all that we had done in three weeks they undid for us in a single day, because in proportion as we dammed up the river on our side they widened it on theirs by the holes they made.

In the place of the sultan, who had died of the illness with which he was seized before the city of Emessa, they had chosen for their chief a Saracen named Scecedin.[1] It was said that the Emperor Frederick had knighted him. This chief gave orders to a part of his forces to attack our army from the Damietta side, which they did, for they crossed the Rexi river at a town called Sharmesah. On Christmas-day I and my knights were dining with Monseigneur Peter d'Avallon, and while we were at dinner they came galloping right up to the camp, and cut to pieces several poor creatures who were wandering about the fields on foot. We hastened to arm ourselves, but were unable to get back soon enough to find Monseigneur Peter, our host, who was already out of the camp and on his way to oppose the Saracens. We spurred after him, and rescued him from the Saracens, who had pulled him to the ground, and we brought him back to the camp, together with his brother, the Seigneur de Val. The Templars, who had sallied out at the first alarm, covered our retreat bravely and skilfully; but the Turks harassed us right up to our camp, wherefore the king gave orders to enclose our camp with ditches from the Damietta side to the Rexi river.

---

[1] The Emir Fahr-eddin, son of the sheik Sadr-eddin.

Scecedin, whose name I have already mentioned, was the most esteemed of all the paynim. On his banners he bore the arms of the emperor who had knighted him. His banner was striped, and on one of the stripes were the arms of the emperor who made him a knight, on another the arms of the Sultan of Aleppo, and on the third those of the Sultan of Babylon. He was named Scecedin, the son of the sheik, which means the old man, son of the old man. This title is looked upon as one of great consequence among the paynim, for of all the peoples in the world they the most highly honour aged persons, when they find that God has preserved them from dishonourable imputations unto their old age. Scecedin, that valiant Turk, as the king's spies brought word, boasted that he would dine on St. Sebastian's day (January 20th) in the king's tents.

The king, who was aware of this, disposed his army so that the Count of Artois his brother should guard the "Cats" and the engines; the king and the Count of Anjou, who was afterwards king of Sicily, were posted to protect the camp on the side towards Babylon; while the Count of Poitiers and we others from Champagne were to guard the camp on the side towards Damietta. And it came to pass that the above-named prince of the Turks made his people cross over into the island which lies between the rivers of Damietta and Rexi, where our army was encamped, and he drew up his battalions from one river to the other. The King of Sicily attacked these troops and discomfited them. Many of them were drowned in both rivers, but yet a large force of them remained whom the king dared not attack, because the engines of the Saracens commanded the space between the two rivers. In the attack which the King of Sicily made upon the Turks, the Count Guy of Forez passed

E

right through the Turkish army on horseback, and at the head of his knights charged a battalion of Saracen sergeants, who threw him to the ground; and he had one of his legs broken, and two of his knights brought him back in their arms. It was with great difficulty that the King of Sicily was extricated from the danger in which he had placed himself, and he was much esteemed for that day's work.

The Turks came against the Count of Poitiers and us, and we charged and pursued them some distance. Some of their people were killed, but we returned without losing any.

One evening when we were on duty near the Cats' castles they brought against us an engine called *pierrière*,[1] which they had never done before, and they placed Greek fire in the sling of the engine. When Monseigneur Walter de Cureil, the good knight, who was with me, saw that, he said to us :—

" Sirs, we are in the greatest peril we have yet been in; for if they set fire to our towers, and we remain here, we are dead men, and if we leave our posts which have been entrusted to us, we are put to shame; and no one can save us from this peril save God. It is therefore my opinion and my advice to you, that each time they discharge the fire at us we should throw ourselves upon our elbows and knees, and pray our Lord to bring us out of this danger."

As soon as they fired, we threw ourselves upon our elbows and knees as he had counselled us. The first shot they fired came between our two Cats' castles, and fell in front of us on the open place which the army had made for the purpose of damming the river. Our

---

[1] Literally, a quarry, intended to discharge stones.

men whose duty it was to extinguish fires were all ready
for it ; and because the Saracens could not aim at them
on account of the two wings of the sheds which the king
had erected there, they fired straight up towards the
clouds, so that their darts came down from above upon
them. The nature of the Greek fire was in this wise, that
it rushed forward as large round as a cask of verjuice,
and the tail of the fire which issued from it was as big
as a large-sized spear. It made such a noise in coming
that it seemed as if it were a thunderbolt from heaven,
and looked like a dragon flying through the air. It cast
such a brilliant light that in the camp they could see as
clearly as if it were daytime, because of the light dif-
fused by such a bulk of fire. Three times that night
they discharged the Greek fire at us, and four times
they sent it from the fixed cross-bows. Each time that
our sainted king heard that they had discharged the
Greek fire at us, he dressed himself on his bed and
stretched out his hands towards our Lord, and prayed
with tears : "Fair Sire God, preserve me my people!"
And I verily believe that his prayers stood us in good
stead in our hour of need. That evening, every time
the fire fell, he sent one of his chamberlains to inquire
in what state we were, and if the fire had done us any
damage. One time they threw it, it fell close to the
Cats' castle which Monseigneur de Courtenay's people
were guarding, and struck on the river bank. Then
a knight named l'Aubigoiz called to me and said :—

"Sir, if you do not help us, we are all burnt, for the
Saracens have discharged so many of their darts dipped
in Greek fire, that there is of them as it were a great
blazing hedge coming towards our tower."

We ran forward and hastened thither, and found that
he spoke the truth. We extinguished the fire, but be-

fore we had done so the Saracens covered us with the
darts they discharged from the other side of the river.

The king's brothers mounted guard on the roof of the
Cats' castles to fire bolts from cross-bows against the
Saracens, and which fell into their camp. The king had
commanded that when the King of Sicily mounted guard
in the daytime at the Cats' castles, we were to do so at night.
One day that the King of Sicily was keeping watch,
which we should have to do at night, we were in much
trouble of mind because the Saracens had shattered our
Cats' castles. The Saracens brought out the *pierrière* in
the daytime, which they had hitherto done only at night,
and discharged the Greek fire at our towers. They had
approached their engines so near to the causeway which
the army had constructed to dam the river that no one
dared to go to the towers, because of the huge stones
which the engines flung upon the road. The consequence
of which was that our two towers were burnt, and the
King of Sicily was so wild about it, that he was like to
fling himself into the fire to extinguish it. But if he
were wrathful, I and my knights, for our part, gave
thanks to God; for if we had mounted guard at night,
we should have been all burnt.

When the king saw that, he summoned all the barons
and begged them to give him the timber of their vessels
to make a " Cat" to dam the river. He pointed out to
them very clearly that there was no wood to make it with
except the timber of the vessels that had brought our
armour up the river. They gave what seemed good to
each, and when the " Cat" was finished the timber was
valued at upwards of 10,000 livres.

The king also ruled that the " Cat" should not be
brought upon the embankment until the day came on
which the King of Sicily was to keep watch, to remedy

the mishap that had befallen the other Cats' castles
which were burnt during his watch. As it was ruled, so
was it done ; and as soon as the King of Sicily came
upon his post, he caused the "Cat" to be moved up to
the spot where the two Cats' castles had been burnt.
When the Saracens saw it, they so managed that all their
sixteen machines fired upon the embankment where the
"Cat" had been placed. And when they perceived that
our people feared to go to the "Cat" by reason of the
stones from the engines which fell upon the embankment,
they brought up the *pierrière*, and discharged Greek fire
at the "Cat" until it was burnt to the ground. It was a
great mercy which God showed to me and my knights,
for we should have kept the night watch in as great peril
as we should have done at the other watch, of which I
have before spoken.

When the king saw that, he summoned all his barons
to take counsel together. Then they agreed among
themselves that they would never be able to make an
embankment by which they could pass over to the
Saracens, because our people were unable to dam up as
much on the one side as the Saracens widened on the
other. Thereupon the Constable, Monseigneur Imbert
de Beaujeu, told the king that a Bedaween had come and
said that he could point out a good ford, provided they
would give him 500 bezants. The king said he would
agree to give them to him if he fulfilled what he promised. The constable spoke on the subject to the
Bedaween, who said that he would not show the ford
unless they paid him the money in advance. It was
agreed that it should be handed over to him, and it was
done.

The king decided that the Duke of Burgundy and the
rich men from foreign parts who were in the camp should

guard it and save it from harm; and that the king and his three brothers should cross at the ford which the Bedaween was to point out. This enterprise was arranged to come off on the Mardi-Gras (Shrove Tuesday), on which day we came to the Bedaween's ford. As the day broke we made ready at all points, and when all was ready we rode into the river, and our horses were out of their depth. But when we had reached mid-stream we found bottom, and our horses were able to wade; and on the river bank we observed about 300 Saracens on horseback.

Then I said to my people: "Sirs, look only to the left, and let every one turn that way; the banks are rotten, and horses falling upon their riders will drown them."

And it was very true that several were drowned in crossing over, and among others, Monseigneur John d'Orleans, who carried a banner *vivrée*. We managed so that we turned against the current of the stream, and found the way clear, and crossed in such wise that, thank God, not one of us fell in; and as soon as we were over, the Turks took to flight.

Orders had been given that the Temple should form the advanced guard, and that the Count of Artois should have the second division next to the Templars. But it so chanced that as soon as the Count of Artois had crossed the river, he and his people rushed at the Turks, who were fleeing before them. The Templars called out to him that he was offering them a great affront in going before them, when he ought to go behind, and they asked him to let them take the lead, as the king had ordered. But the Count of Artois was afraid to answer them because of Monseigneur Foucault de Merle, who held the bridle of his horse; and this Foucault de Merle, an excellent knight, did not hear a word of what the Templars said to the count, for he was deaf; and he kept shouting, " At them! at them!" When the Templars saw that, they judged that they would be disgraced if they let the Count of Artois go before them; so they spurred on as fast as they could, and pursued the Turks, who fled before them, right through the town of Mansourah to the fields lying close to Babylon. When they thought of returning, the Turks threw down upon them beams and javelins in the narrow streets. There were slain the Count of Artois, the Sire de Coucy, named Raoul, and so many other knights, that they were reckoned at 300. The Temple, as I have been told, lost there 280 men-at-arms, and all on horseback.

Myself and my knights resolved to attack a body of Turks who were loading their baggage in the camp on our left hand, and accordingly went at them. While we were chasing them through the camp, I noticed a Saracen mounting a horse, whose bridle was held by one of his knights. Just as he put his two hands on the saddle to mount, I struck him with my lance below the arm-pit, and sent him down a dead man. When his knight saw that, he left his lord and his horse, and struck me as I passed between the shoulders with his lance, and bent me over the neck of my horse, and held me so tight that I could not draw the sword which I carried at my belt, so that I was obliged to draw the sword which was attached to my horse, and when he observed that I had drawn my sword, he drew out his lance and left me. As I and my knights came out of the Saracens' camp we encountered fully 6000 Turks, as we reckoned, who had left their quarters and were retreating across the plains. As soon as they saw us they came straight at us, and slew Monseigneur Hugh de Trichatel, Seigneur de Conflans, who bore my banner. I and my knights clapped spurs to our horses and went to rescue Monseigneur Raoul de Wanou, who was in my company, and whom they had overthrown. As I was returning the Turks struck me with their lances, my horse fell on his knees beneath the burden he felt, and I shot forward over his ears. I gained my feet, with my shield round my neck and sword in hand, when Monseigneur Erard de Siverey (whom may God absolve), who was near me, came up to me and proposed that we should retire towards a house in ruins, and there await the king, who was approaching. While we were on our way thither, one on foot and one on horseback, a large body of Turks rushed upon us, threw me to the ground, passed over me, and made my shield fly from my neck. And when they had passed on, Monseigneur Erard de Siverey came back to me, and brought me on, and we went together until we reached the house in ruins. There we were joined by Monseigneur Hugh d'Escoz, Monseigneur Frederick de Loupey, and Monseigneur Reginald de Menoncourt. The Turks now attacked us on all sides. Some of them entered the ruined house, and thrust at us with their spears from above. Then my knights told me to hold their horses by the bridle, for fear they should gallop away, and I did so; and they defended themselves against the Turks so vigorously that they were praised by all the brave men in the army, both by those who witnessed their prowess and by those who heard it spoken of. There Monseigneur Hugh d'Escoz was wounded by three lance-thrusts in the face, and Monseigneur Raoul, and Monseigneur Frederick de Loupey received a lance-thrust between his shoulders, and the wound was so broad that the blood gushed from his body as through the bunghole of a cask. Monseigneur Erard de Siverey was wounded in the face by a sword, so that his nose fell upon his lip. Then I bethought me of Monseigneur St. James : "Fair Sir St. James, to whom I pray, help and succour me in this need." I had hardly finished my prayer when Monseigneur Erard de Siverey said to me : " Sir, if you think that neither I nor my heirs would incur reproach, I would go and seek succour for you from the Count of Anjou, whom I see there in the midst of the fields."

And I answered, "Sir Erard, it seems to me that you would do yourself much honour if you would go in quest of aid to save our lives, for your own is also in great peril." And I spoke truly, for he died of his wound. Then he consulted the other knights who were there, all of whom approved of the advice I had given him. When he heard that, he asked me to let go his horse, which I held with the others, and I did so. He went to the Count of Anjou, and begged him to come to the rescue of myself and my knights. A rich man who was with him tried to dissuade him, but the count told him he would do what my knight requested, and he turned his horse's head to come to our aid, and some of his sergeants spurred forward. When the Saracens beheld them, they quitted us. In advance of these sergeants came Monseigneur Peter d'Auberive, sword in hand, and when they saw that the Saracens had left us, they charged a body of the enemy who had taken Monseigneur Raoul de Wanou, and delivered him out of their hands sorely wounded. While I was on foot with my knights, and wounded as I have already described, there came the king with the whole of his division, with loud shouts, and much noise of trumpets and cymbals, and he halted upon a raised causeway. Never have I seen so fine a knight, for he towered above

all his people, out-topping them by the shoulders, a
gilded helmet on his head, and a German sword in his
hand. When he halted there, the good knights whom
he had about his person, and whom I have already
named, dashed into the midst of the Turks, with many
other valiant knights who were in the king's own
" battle." And it was truly a fine passage of arms, for
no one drew bow or cross-bow, but it was a combat
with sword and mace between the Turks and our people,
who were all mingled together. One of my squires
who had fled with my banner, and had returned to me,
brought me one of my horses, upon which I mounted
and went to the king, close by his side. While we were
thus together, Monseigneur John de Valery, a man of
worth, came to the king, and said that he would advise
him to bear to the right towards the river so as to have
the aid of the Duke of Burgundy, and the others who
were guarding the camp which we had left, and to
enable his men to slake their thirst, for the heat was
already very great. The king commanded his sergeants
to go and seek his good knights, whom he kept about
his person as advisers, and whose names he repeated.
The sergeants went in quest of them, in the midst of
the *mêlée*, where the strife was fierce between them and
the Turks. When they came to the king, he asked
their advice, and they said that Monseigneur John de
Valery had given him good counsel. Whereupon the
king commanded that the oriflamme of St. Denis and
his other banners should be borne to the right towards
the river. When the king's army put itself in motion,
there was again a great noise of trumpets and Saracen
horns. He had scarcely moved, however, when he
received several messages from his brother, the Count
of Poitiers, the Count of Flanders, and many other

rich men who had their troops there, praying him not
to move, for they were so pressed by the Turks that
they could not follow him. The king again called together all the valiant knights his counsellors, and all
were of opinion that he should stay where he was; but
a little afterwards, Monseigneur John de Valery came
back and blamed the king and his counsellors for halting. After a while, all were agreed that he should bear
towards the river, as the Sire de Valery had recommended. At that moment, the Constable Monseigneur
Imbert de Baujeu came to him and said that his brother,
the Count of Artois, was defending himself in a house
at Mansourah, and that he was going to succour him.
Then the king said to him: "Constable, lead the way,
and I will follow." I, too, said to the constable that I
would be his knight, and he thanked me heartily. We
set out to go to Mansourah. Presently a mace-sergeant
came up to the constable, all dismayed, and said that
the king had halted, and that the Turks had got between
him and us. We turned round and saw that there were
a thousand or more between him and ourselves; and
there were only six of us. Then I said to the constable: "Sir, we cannot make our way to the king
through these people, so let us go up the river and
place that ditch you see yonder between us and them,
and by that means we shall be able to rejoin the king."
The constable did as I advised him; and, assuredly, had
they taken heed of us, we should all have been slain,
but they thought only of the king, and the other heavy
battalions, and thus fancied that we were of their
side.

While we were descending the river on the bank
between it and the streamlet, we saw that the king
had approached the river, and that the Turks were

pushing back the other battalions, smiting them with
mighty strokes of sword and mace, and they drove back
upon the river all the other corps, as well as the king's
own. The discomfiture was at that moment so great,
that some of our people attempted to cross over by
swimming to the side where the Duke of Burgundy
was, which they did not succeed in doing, for their
horses were done up, and the heat was very great, so
that we saw, as we were coming down, that the river
was dotted over with spears and shields, and with horses
and men who were sinking and perishing. We came
to a little bridge over the stream, when I said to the
constable that we ought to stop to guard this bridge,
"for if we leave it open they will throw themselves
upon the king from this side, and if our people are
attacked from two quarters at once they are like to
give way." And we did so. And it was said that it
would have been all up with us that day had not the
king been present in person. For the Sire de Courtenay and Monseigneur John de Saillenay described to
me how six Turks seized the king's horse by the bridle,
and were leading him away prisoner, but he delivered
himself from them single handed, by the mighty sword-
strokes he dealt them. And when his people saw the
defence the king made, they plucked up courage, and
left off crossing over the river, and returned towards
the king to aid him.

Straight towards us rode Count Peter of Brittany,
who had come direct from Mansourah, and was wounded
with a sword-cut in the face, so that the blood ran into
his mouth. He was on a short strong-limbed horse,
and had thrown his reins upon his saddle-bow, to which
he clung with both hands, fearing lest his people,
who were coming up behind and pressing him close,

might hustle him out of his seat. He seemed to prize them but little, for when he had spat the blood out of his mouth, he said: "Ho! by God's head! Have you ever seen such rascals?" Behind his corps came the Count of Soissons and Monseigneur Peter de Neuville, called Caier, who had had their share of blows that day. When they had crossed over, and the Turks perceived that we were guarding the bridge, they left them because they saw we were ready to face them. I went up to the Count of Soissons, whose cousin-german I had married, and said to him: "Sir, I think you would do well if you would stop to defend this bridge, for, if we leave it, the Turks you see in front of you will dash over, and the king will be assailed both behind and in front." He asked me if, in the event of his stopping, I would stop too; and I replied, "Yes, very willingly." When the constable heard that, he bade me not to move from thence until he returned, for he was going in quest of succour.

So there I remained upon my back, with the Count of Soissons on my right hand, and Monseigneur Peter de Neuville on the left. Then a Turk came behind us, from hovering about the king's division, and, from be-hind, struck Monseigneur Peter de Neuville with a mace, and made him bend over his horse's neck with the force of the blow, after which he dashed over the bridge, and rejoined his own people. When the Turks saw that we would not abandon the bridge, they crossed the stream, and placed themselves between it and the river, as we had done to come down. And we bore ourselves towards them, so that we were ready to charge them if they attempted either to pass towards the king, or to cross the bridge.

In front of us were two of the king's sergeants, of

whom one was named William de Boon, the other John de Gamaches, against whom the Turks, who had got between the stream and the river, brought a number of common fellows on foot, who pelted them with clods of earth, but they were unable to throw them as far as to us. At last they brought a foot soldier who, three times, discharged Greek fire at them; and one time William de Boon received the pot of Greek fire on his shield: had anything about him caught fire, he would have been burnt to death. We were stuck all over with darts which had missed the sergeants. It chanced that I found a quilted vest upon a Saracen; I turned the open side towards myself, and made a shield of it, of which I stood in great need, for I was wounded by their darts in five places, and my back in fifteen. It happened also that one of my Joinville burghers brought me a banner pointed with steel, and whenever we saw that they were pressing the sergeants too hard, we charged them, and they fled a space.

The good Count of Soissons, notwithstanding the straits we were in, jested with me and said: "Seneschal, let those curs howl, for *par la Coiffe-dieu* (his favourite oath), we shall live to speak of this day in ladies' bowers."

In the evening, towards sunset, the constable brought us the king's crossbowmen on foot, who drew themselves up in front of us, and when the Saracens saw them put foot to the stirrup of their crossbows, they took to flight. Then the seneschal said to me: "Seneschal, it is well done; so go you to the king, and don't quit his side until he has alighted at his tent." Soon after I had rejoined the king, Monseigneur John de Valery came to him and said: " Sire, Monseigneur de Châtillon begs that you will give him the rearguard." The king did so very gladly, and then set out. As we were going along, I made him take off his helmet, and lent to him my iron skull cap, so that he might get some air. Then came up to him brother Henry de Ronnay, who had crossed the river, and kissed his gauntleted hand. The king asked him if he had any tidings of his brother, the Count of Artois, and he replied that he had very good news of him, for he was quite certain that he was in Paradise. " Ah, Sire, be of good cheer, for such great honour never alighted upon any King of France as has alighted upon you, for, in order to combat your enemies, you have crossed a river by swimming, and have discomfited and driven them from the field of battle, and have captured their engines and tents, in which you will sleep this night." Whereupon the king said that God should be praised for the good gifts He gave, and then big tears fell from his eyes.

When we reached the camp, we saw some Saracens on foot holding on to a tent which they had struck, while some of our attendants were tugging at it on the other side. The master of the Temple and myself dashed at them: but they fled and left the tent with our people.

In this battle there were some people of great pretensions, who came out of it with much dishonour, fleeing over the little bridge of which mention has been made, and fleeing in such terror that we could not prevail upon one of them to remain with us. I could easily name them; but abstain from doing so, seeing that they are dead.

But of Monseigneur Guyon Mauvoisin I will not abstain from speaking, for he came from Mansourah with honour, and he went down the river as far as the constable and I went up it; and as the Turks drove back the Count of Brittany and his corps, so did they force back Monseigneur Guyon Mauvoisin and his corps: he and his people won great honour that day. Nor was it surprising that he and his people should have borne themselves well, for those who knew all about it, told me that his corps was almost entirely composed of knights of his own lineage, and of knights who were his liegemen.

When we had discomfited the Turks, and chased them out of their tents, and while none of our people were there, the Bedaweens flung themselves into the camp, and they were in great numbers. They left nothing whatever in the camp, but carried off whatever the Saracens had left; and I never heard it said that the Bedaweens, who are subjects of the Saracens, were thought the worse of by them for what they took or stole, because it is their custom and usage always to attack the weakest.

CHAPTER VI.

S it belongs to my subject, I will tell you what sort of people are the Bedaweens. The Bedaweens do not believe in Mohammed, but in the law of Ali,[1] who was Mohammed's uncle. They also believe in the Old Man of the Mountain, who maintains the Assassins. They believe, too, that when a man dies for his lord, or with a good intention, his soul passes into a better and happier form than before, wherefore the Assassins think little of taking life when executing the orders of the Old Man of the Mountain. For the present we will pass over the Old Man of the Mountain, and will speak of the Bedaweens.

The Bedaweens live neither in villages nor in towns, nor yet in castles, but dwell always in the plains. They place their households, their wives and children, either for the night, or, in bad weather, for the day, in a sort of hut, which they make with hoops fastened to poles, like ladies' cars; and upon these hoops they lay sheep-skins, called Damascus skins, dressed with alum. The Bedaweens themselves wear loose cloaks made of these,

---

[1] Ali was cousin and son in-law to Mohammed.

r

which cover the whole body, legs, and feet. When it rains in the evening, or the weather is bad at night, they wrap themselves up in their cloaks, take the bridles off their horses, and let them feed close by. When the morning comes, they lay out their cloaks in the sun and give them a dressing, after which there is nothing about them to show that they were soaked over night. Their belief is that no one can die before his time, and therefore they refuse to put on armour, and when they curse their children, they say to them: "Be thou accursed as the Frank, who puts on armour from fear of death." In battle they carry nothing but sword and spear. Nearly all of them are clad in white robes, like priests; towels are twisted round their heads, and pass under their chins, which makes them ugly and hideous to look at, for the hair of their head and beard is quite black. They live on the milk of their animals, and purchase from rich men the pasturages in the desert, on which their flocks are fed.

Their number nobody can tell, for they are found in the kingdom of Egypt, in the kingdom of Jerusalem, and in all the other lands of the Saracens, and infidels, to whom they pay large tribute every year.

I have seen in this country, since I came back from beyond sea, several disloyal Christians who held the belief of the Bedaweens, and said that none could die before his day; but their faith is so disloyal, that it might as well be said that God has no power to help us, for they who serve God would be very foolish if they did not believe that He has power to prolong their lives, and to save them from harm and accident; so ought we to believe that He has power to do everything.

Now let us tell how, at night, we returned from that perilous battle, the king and the rest of us, and lodged

in the spot whence we had dislodged the enemy. My
people, who had remained in the camp whence we had
started, brought me a tent, given to me by the Templars, and pitched it in front of the engines which we
had captured from the Saracens; and the king posted
sergeants to guard the engines. I had lain down on
my bed, where I had much need of rest because of the
wounds I had received in the day-time; but that rest
was not to be had, for, before it was daylight, there
were shouts in our camp of "To arms! To arms!" I
made my chamberlain get up, who was lying in front of
me, and told him to go and see what was the matter.
He came back all in a fright, and cried out, "Sir, up!
up! The Saracens have come, both foot and horse, and
have discomfited the king's sergeants who were guarding
the engines, and have driven them back to our tent-
ropes." I sprang up, and threw a quilted vest over my
back, and placed an iron skull-cap upon my head, and
shouted to our sergeants: "By St. Nicholas, they shall
not remain here!" My knights came to me, all wounded
as they were, and we drove back the Saracen sergeants
away from the engines, and up to a heavy body of
mounted Turks, who were over against the machines
we had taken. I sent to the king to succour us, for
neither myself nor my knights could put on our hauberks, because of the wounds we had received. And
the king dispatched to us Monseigneur Walter de Châtillon, who took up his post in front of us, between us
and the Turks.

When the Sire de Châtillon had repulsed the foot
sergeants of the Saracens, they retreated towards a
heavy body of mounted Turks, who were drawn up in
front of our camp to prevent us from surprising the
army of the Saracens which was encamped in their

rear.   Of this body of mounted Turks, eight of their
leaders, well armed, had dismounted, and made a barri-
cade of hewn stones, so that our crossbowmen should
not wound them.   These eight Saracens fired at random
into our camp, and wounded many of our men and
horses.   I and my knights held a conference, and
arranged that when night was come we would carry off
the stones behind which they had barricaded themselves.
A priest who was with me, named Monseigneur John
de Voysset, was at this counsel, but did not wait so
long. Going out of our camp all alone, he went straight
towards the Saracens, clad in a quilted vest, with an
iron skull-cap on his head, and a lance, the point of
which trailed under his arm, so that it might not be
seen by the Saracens. When he had come near to the
Saracens, for they took no notice of him as being only
a solitary individual, he drew the lance out from under
his arm, and rushed at them : not one of the eight stood
on his defence, but all took to flight together.   When
the mounted Saracens observed their chiefs running
away, they spurred forward to rescue them, and there
issued from our camp some fifty of the king's sergeants.
And the mounted Saracens galloped up, but did not
venture to engage in combat with our foot-soldiers, and
wheeled about.   When they had done that two or three
times, one of our sergeants grasped his spear by the
middle, and, hurling it at one of the mounted Turks,
pierced him between the ribs.   When the Turks saw
that, they no longer dared to skirmish around them,
and our sergeants carried away the stones.   From that
time my priest was well known in the camp, and they
used to point him out to one another, and say : "That
is Monseigneur de Joinville's priest, who discomfited the
eight Saracens."

These events happened in the first week in Lent (A. D. 1250). That same day a valiant Saracen whom our enemies had appointed their leader in the room of Sceeedin, the son of the Sheik, whom they had lost in the fight on Shrove-Tuesday, took the Count of Artois' coat of arms, who had also been killed in that battle, and showed it to all the host of the Saracens, and told them it was the king's coat of arms, and that he was slain.

" I show you this," said he, " because a body without a head is not to be feared, nor a people without their king. Therefore, if it so please you, let us attack them on Friday or Saturday, and it seems to me that you ought not to hesitate, for we cannot fail to take them all, now that they have lost their head." And all agreed that they would assault us on the Friday.

The king's spies who were in the Saracens' camp brought these tidings to the king, who thereupon commanded all the leaders of battalions to arm their people by midnight, and march them out from the tents to the open space outside, which was fortified by long stakes of wood to check the inroads of the Saracens, and these stakes were so driven into the ground that a man could pass between them on foot. According to the king's commands so was it done.

Just as the sun was rising the Saracen whom they had chosen as their chief brought against us 4000 mounted Turks, whom he drew up round our camp, from the river that comes from Babylon to the one that flowed from our camp towards a town named Rexi. When this was done, they brought up such a swarm of foot-soldiers that they surrounded our camp a second time. Behind these two bodies of troops they arrayed all the forces of the Sultan of Babylon to support them, if need were. When they had done that, the chief rode forward upon a small hack to note the disposition of our camp, and wherever he observed our battalions were stronger at one point than another, he returned to his own people and reinforced the battalions opposed to ours.   After that he made the Bedaweens, some 3000 in number, pass over between the two rivers ; and this he did because he fancied that the king would detach a portion of his men and send them to aid the Duke of Burgundy against the Bedaweens, by which the king's army would have been so far enfeebled.

It took him till noon to make these arrangements, and then he ordered his cymbals to clash, whereupon his people rushed at us on foot and on horseback. I will speak to you first of the King of Sicily, who was at that time Count of Anjou, because he was first on the Babylon side.   They came at him as if they were playing a game of chess, for they attacked him with their foot-soldiers, and these flung Greek fire at him ; and the horsemen and footmen pressed forward so that they discomfited the King of Sicily, who was in the midst of his knights on foot.   And one went to the king and told him of the danger his brother was in.   When he heard that, he spurred forward through the midst of his brother's troops, sword in hand, and rushed in among the Turks so far that they threw Greek fire upon his horse's crupper. By this deed of arms the king succoured the King of Sicily and his people, and they drove the Turks out of their camp.

Next to the battalion of the King of Sicily was that of the foreign barons, of whom Messire Guy d'Ibelin and Messire Baldwin, his brother, were leaders.   And next to them came the corps of Monseigneur Walter de Châtillon, full of men of worth and chivalry. These two corps defended themselves so vigorously that the Turks

failed either to pierce them or to force them back. Next
to the corps of Monseigneur Walter stood brother William de Sonnac, Master of the Temple, with the handful
of knights that remained to him after the battle of
Shrove-Tuesday. He had constructed defences in front
of his position with the engines we had taken from the
Saracens. When these came forward to attack him they
cast Greek fire upon the stockade he had made, and it
caught immediately, for the Templars had worked in
great planks of firwood. Be sure the Turks did not
wait till the fire had burnt out, but rushed in at the
Templars through the flames. In this battle, brother
William, the Master of the Temple, lost an eye, the
other one he lost on Shrove-Tuesday; and of this he died,
and may God absolve him. Behind the Templars there
was a piece of ground as large as a man could till in one
day, which was stuck so full of the darts thrown by the
Saracens that you scarcely saw the ground by reason of
the quantity of javelins.

Next to the Temple corps was that of Monseigneur
Guyon de Mauvoisin, which the Turks never could
overcome; and yet it happened that they covered Monseigneur Guyon de Mauvoisin with Greek fire, which
was extinguished with great difficulty.

From the spot where was posted the battalion of Monseigneur Guyon de Mauvoisin the palisade which surrounded our army turned in towards the river to within
a moderate stone's-throw. From that point it passed in
front of the division of Count William of Flanders, and
extended as far as the river which flows towards the sea.
Upon a line drawn from Monseigneur Guyon de Mauvoisin our battalion was stationed; but because the
corps of Count William of Flanders confronted the
Saracens, they never ventured to come at us; in which

God showed us great favour, for neither I nor my knights had either hauberks or shields, because we had all been wounded in the battle on Shrove-Tuesday.

They charged the Count of Flanders hotly and vigorously, both horse and foot; but when I saw that, I bade our crossbowmen fire upon the horsemen. When the mounted Saracens found that they were being wounded from our side, they took to flight; and when this was seen by the count's people they left the camp, leaped over the palisade, rushed at the Saracen infantry, and discomfited them. Several of them were killed, and many of their bucklers were taken. There Walter de la Horgne, who bore the banner of Monseigneur d'Apremont, acquitted himself right valiantly.

Next to the corps of the Count of Flanders came the corps of the Count of Poitiers, the king's brother, which corps was on foot, the count alone being on horseback. This corps the Turks utterly routed, and were carrying off the Count of Poitiers a prisoner; but when the butchers and other men about the camp and the women who sold wares heard of that, they gave the alarm throughout the camp, and with God's help the count was rescued and the Turks expelled from the camp.

Next to the corps of the Count of Poitiers was posted that of Monseigneur Josserand de Brancion, who had come into Egypt with the count, and was one of the best knights in the army. He had so disposed his men that all his knights were on foot, but he himself was on horseback, with his son Monseigneur Henry, and the son of Monseigneur Josserand de Nanton: these he kept on horseback because they were mere youths. More than once the Turks discomfited his people, and each time that he saw this he spurred on and charged the Turks from the rear, when the Turks left his people

to attack himself. However, that would not have prevented the Turks from leaving them all dead upon the
field of battle, had it not been for Monseigneur Henry
de Cône, who was in the camp of the Duke of Burgundy, a sagacious knight, valiant and thoughtful. Each
time that he observed the Turks fall upon Monseigneur
de Brancion he made the king's crossbowmen fire upon
the Turks across the river. In any case the Sire de
Brancion escaped the perils of that day ; but of twenty
knights he had with him he lost twelve, without reckoning the other men-at-arms. He himself was so mal-
treated that he was never again able to stand upon his
feet, and he died of the wounds he had received in
God's service.

I will speak to you of the Seigneur de Brancion. He
had been, before he died, in thirty-six battles and com-
bats, in all of which he had carried off the prize of
valour. I saw him in an expedition of the Count of
Châlons, whose cousin he was. He came up to myself
and my brother one Good Friday, and said : "My
nephews, come and help me, you and your people, for
the Germans are breaking everything in the church."

We went with him and attacked them, sword in hand,
and with much trouble, and after a hard fight, we drove
them out of the church. When this was done the worthy
man knelt down before the altar and cried to our Lord
with a loud voice, and said : "Sire, I pray unto Thee to
have pity upon me, and take me away from these strifes
among Christians, in the midst of which I have lived so
long, and vouchsafe unto me that I may die in Thy
service, so that I may win Thy kingdom of Paradise."
I have told you all this because I believe that God heard
his prayer, as you have seen above.

After the battle of the first Friday in Lent, the king

summoned all his barons to his presence and said to
them: " We owe hearty thanks to our Lord that He
has twice in this week done us so great an honour that
on the Tuesday which precedes Lent we drove them
from their camp in which we are now lodged; and on
the following Friday we, being on foot, defended ourselves against them who were on horseback." And many
other such words did he address unto them to encourage
them.

To follow our matter distinctly, we must mix with
it other matter to explain how the sultans kept
their troops in order and array. It is a fact that
the greater part of their chivalry was composed of
foreigners, whom dealers obtained in foreign lands for
the purpose of selling them; and they purchased them
eagerly, and at a high price. These persons whom the
dealers brought into Egypt they procured in the East,
because when any one of the Eastern kings defeated
another, he took the poor of the people he had con-
quered and sold them to the dealers, and the dealers
went away and sold them into Egypt.

The system was so organized that the sultan brought
up the children in his own house until such time as
their beards began to come, and according to their
strength the sultan had bows made for them, and as they
grew stronger and stronger they deposited their bows in
the sultan's arsenal, and the head of the department
assigned to them bows as stiff as they were able to bend.
The sultan's arms were of gold, and what arms the sultan bore were borne also by these young men, who were
called *bahariz* (people from the sea).

As soon as their beards came the sultan made them
knights. They bore the sultan's arms, with a difference,
to wit, red devices, roses, or red bands, or birds, or such

other devices as they pleased, which they placed upon
a field *or*. They were called *Halca*,[1] for the *baharis*
slept in the sultan's tents. When the sultan was in
camp, the *Halca* were lodged round the sultan's tent,
and appointed to guard his person. At the door of the
sultan's tent were lodged in a small tent the sultan's
doorkeepers and minstrels, the latter playing upon
Saracen horns, drums, and cymbals; and they made
such a noise at daybreak and nightfall that those who
were near them could not hear one another speak; and
they were plainly heard all through the camp. The
minstrels would never venture to play upon their instruments in the day-time without an order from the master
of the *Halca*, whence it happened that when the sultan
wished to give any orders he sent for the master of the
Halca and intimated to him his commands; then the
master caused the sultan's instruments to be sounded,
whereupon the whole army came to receive the sultan's
orders, which the master of the *Halca* repeated, and
which the whole army executed.

When the sultan engaged in battle, the knights of the
Halca, if they acquitted themselves valiantly in the
fight, were made emirs by the sultan, who also assigned
to them companies of two to three hundred knights, and
the more they distinguished themselves the greater the
rewards which the sultan gave them.

The prize reserved for these knights, when they are
so valiant and rich that there is nothing more to be said
about it, and when the sultan is afraid lest they should
slay or dethrone him, is, that he seizes them and leaves
them to perish in his dungeon, and despoils their wives

---

[1] An Arabic word signifying " a circle," " a guard."

of whatever they have. This is what the sultan did to those who made prisoners of the Count of Montfort and the Count of Bar; and so likewise did Bondocdar to those who defeated the King of Armenia; for, expecting to receive a rich guerdon, they dismounted from their horses, and went to salute him while he was at a wild beast hunt. He answered them : " I do not salute you ;" for they had interrupted his hunting, and he cut off their heads.

Let us now return to our story, and tell how the sultan who died left a son, twenty-five years of age, sagacious, cunning, and malicious; and because he feared lest he should dethrone him, he bestowed upon him a kingdom he had in the East. As soon as the sultan was dead the emirs sent for his son, who had no sooner arrived in Egypt than he deprived his father's seneschal, constable, and marshal of their golden rods, and gave them to men who had come with him from the East. When they saw that they felt sorely chagrined, as did all the others who belonged to his father's council, because of the dishonour he had cast upon them. And because they dreaded lest he should do unto them what his grandfather did to those who had taken prisoners the Count of Montfort and the Count of Bar, they intrigued with the *Halca*, whose duty it was to act as the sultan's body guard, until the latter promised at their request to put the sultan to death.

CHAPTER VII.

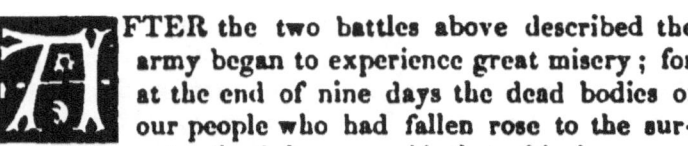

FTER the two battles above described the army began to experience great misery; for at the end of nine days the dead bodies of our people who had fallen rose to the surface of the water (and it was said that this happened because their gall-bladders had putrefied), and they floated to the bridge that joined the two camps, and could not pass through because the bridge rested upon the water. There was such a number of them that the whole surface of the river was covered with dead bodies from one bank to the other, and for the distance of a stone's-throw up the stream. The king engaged a hundred of the camp-followers, who were occupied for eight days. The dead bodies of the Saracens, who were circumcised, they threw over to the other side of the bridge, and let them float down the current; but the Christians they buried in deep trenches, one with another. I saw there the Count of Artois' chamberlains and many others looking for their friends among the dead, but I never heard that any one was identified.

We had no fish in the camp to eat during Lent except the *karmout* (a kind of eel), which preyed upon the dead bodies, for they are a gluttonous fish. And in consequence of this misfortune, and of the unhealthiness of the country, where never a drop of rain falls, we were attacked with the army sickness, which was such that our legs shrivelled up and became covered with black spots, and spots of the colour of earth, like an old boot; and in such of us as fell sick the gums became putrid with sores, and no man recovered of that sickness, but all had to die. It was a sure sign of death when the nose began to bleed: there was nothing left then but to die. About a fortnight afterwards the Turks, in order to starve us out (at which many of our people were astonished), took several of their galleys which were above our camp, dragged them overland to a good league below our camp, and placed them in the river by which supplies came from Damietta. These galleys brought famine upon us, for no one now ventured to come to us from Damietta to bring us provisions by ascending the stream. We knew nothing of all this until a small vessel of the count of Flanders, which fought its way past them, brought us the news, by which time the sultan's galleys had captured eighty of our galleys that were coming from Damietta, and killed all who were on board.

There thence arose such a scarcity in the camp that when Easter had arrived an ox was worth 80 livres, a sheep 30 livres, a pig 30 livres, an egg 12 deniers, and a 60-gallon measure of wine 10 livres.

When the king and the barons saw that, they agreed that the king should withdraw his army from before Babylon, and join the camp of the Duke of Burgundy, which was on the river that goes to Damietta. To effect a junction of his troops with greater safety, the king threw up an outwork before the bridge between the two camps, so that it could be entered on horseback from two sides. As soon as the outwork was completed the king's army was put in array, and the Turks made a fierce assault upon the camp. For all that, neither the camp nor any of the people moved until all the baggage had been carried across then: the king crossed, and with him his division, and after that all the other barons, excepting Monseigneur de Châtillon, who covered the retreat. And at the very moment of entering the outwork, Monseigneur Erard de Valery rescued Monseigneur John, his brother, whom the Turks were carrying off a prisoner.

When the main body of the army had crossed over, those who remained in the outwork were in great danger; for the outwork was not high, so that the Turks on horseback fired at them point-blank, while the Saracens on foot flung clods of earth into their faces. They would all have been cut off had not the Count of Anjou, who was afterwards King of Sicily, gone to their rescue and brought them off safe and sound. The honour of that day fell to Monseigneur Geoffrey de Mussamboure, from out of all who were in the outwork.

On the eve of Shrove-Tuesday I witnessed a wonderful thing, which I should like to recount to you, for on that day was interred Monseigneur Hugh de Landricourt, who was in my company bearing a banner. While he was lying on his bier in my chapel, six of my knights were leaning against some sacks of barley: and because they were talking aloud in my chapel and disturbing the priest with their noise, I went up to them and told them to be silent, and said that it was unbecoming in knights and gentlemen to talk while mass was being chanted. But they only laughed, and answered jestingly that they would find another husband for his widow. Then I rebuked them, and said that such words were neither wise nor witty, and that they had very soon forgotten their comrade. And God took such vengeance for this, that on the morrow, at the great battle of Shrove-Tuesday, they were all killed or mortally wounded; and it happened that all their six wives married a second time.

In consequence of the wounds I had received on Shrove-Tuesday, the army sickness attacked me in the mouth and legs, besides a double tertian fever and so severe a cold in the head that the mucus ran from my nostrils, and on account of these sicknesses, I took to my bed until mid-Lent. My priest therefore chanted the mass in my tent in front of my bed, and he, too, had the same illness. Whence it came to pass that while in the act of consecrating the elements, he turned faint. Seeing that he was like to fall, I, who had put on my tunic, sprang out of bed barefooted, and held him in my arms, and told him to complete the consecration leisurely and properly, for that I would not let go of him until he had finished. He soon recovered himself, completed the consecration, and finished chanting the mass to the end; but he never chanted it again.

After these things the counsellors of the king and of the sultan appointed a day for a conference. The following conditions were agreed to :—That Damietta should be restored to the sultan, who should give up to the king the kingdom of Jerusalem; and the sultan was to take charge of the sick who were at Damietta, and the salted meat (for they never touch pork), and the king's engines, until such time as he should send for them all. Then they asked the king's counsellors what security they would give that Damietta should be restored. The king's counsellors proposed that they should detain one of the king's brothers, either the

Count of Anjou or the Count of Poitiers, until the restoration of Damietta. The Saracens replied that they would make no treaty unless the king's own person was left with them in pledge ; whereupon Monseigneur Geoffrey de Sargines, the good knight, declared that he would rather that the Saracens should take or kill them to a man, than that he should ever hear himself reproached with having left the king in pledge.

The sickness became much more severe throughout the camp, and the proud flesh in our men's mouths grew to such excess that the barber-surgeons were obliged to cut it off, to give them a chance of chewing their food or swallowing anything. It was piteous to hear through the camp the shrieks of the people who were being operated upon for proud flesh, for they shrieked like women in childbirth.

When the king perceived that he could remain there no longer without himself and his people all perishing, he gave orders and instructions for setting out on Tuesday evening, at nightfall, after the octave of Easter, with the intention of returning to Damietta. The king commanded Jocelyn de Cornaut, his brothers, and the other engineers, to sever the ropes which fastened the bridges between us and the Saracens ; but they did not. We embarked on the Tuesday in the afternoon, after dinner, I and the two knights who remained to me of all my company. When the hour of nightfall arrived I bade the mariners raise the anchor and let us float down with the stream ; but they said they dared not, because the sultan's galleys which were between us and Damietta would put us to death. The mariners had kindled large fires to gather the sick to their galleys, and the latter had drawn down to the bank of the river. While I was entreating the ship's people to start, the

G

Saracens broke into the camp, and I saw by the light of the fires that they were slaughtering the sick by the river-side. While my mariners were raising the anchor, those whose duty it was to bring off the sick cut the ropes of their anchors and galleys, and came down upon our small vessels, pressing us so close together that they narrowly missed sending us to the bottom. When we had got clear of this danger, and were dropping down the river, the king, who was suffering much from the army sickness and from dysentery, could have saved himself on board the galleys had he pleased, but he answered that, please God, he would not quit his people. In the evening he fainted several times. They cried out to us who were on the river to wait for the king, and when we refused to wait they fired upon us with bolts, wherefore we were obliged to wait until they should give us permission to set sail.

I will now tell you how the king was made prisoner, as he himself related it to me. He said that he had left his own division, and, together with Monseigneur Geoffrey de Sargines, had joined the corps of Monseigneur Walter de Châtillon, which formed the rear-guard. And the king said that he was mounted on a little hack, with a housing of silk, and that behind him of all his knights and sergeants there remained only Monseigneur Geoffrey de Sargines, who conducted the king to the village in which he was taken; and the king told me that Monseigneur Geoffrey de Sargines defended him against the Saracens just as a good valet drives away the flies from his master's cup; for each time the Saracens drew near he clapped his spear—which he carried between himself and the saddle-bow—under his arm, and charged them and drove them away from the king. And in this manner he brought him on to the village, and they car-

ried the king into a house, and laid him all but dead in
the lap of a woman of the burgher class from Paris,
and they thought he would not hold out till the evening.
Thither came Monseigneur Philip de Montfort, and said
to the king that he saw the emir with whom he had negotiated for a truce, and that, if he pleased, he would
go to him and conclude the truce upon the terms demanded by the Saracens. The king prayed him to go,
for that he much wished it. He went to the Saracen,
who took off his turban from his head and the ring from
his finger, as a pledge that he would keep faith. In the
meanwhile a great misfortune befell our people, for a
traitor sergeant, named Marcel, began to call out to
them: "Sir knights, yield yourselves, for such is the
king's pleasure, and do not cause the king to be put to
death." All believed that such was the king's command, and surrendered their swords to the Saracens.
The emir observed that the Saracens were leading our
people away captive. Then he said to Monseigneur
Philip that it was not fitting that he should accord a
truce to our people, for he saw that they were prisoners.
Thus it happened to Monseigneur Philip that all our
people were prisoners excepting himself, because he was
an envoy. Now, there is a bad custom in the country of
the Paynim, which is, that when the king sends messengers to the sultan, or the sultan to the king, and either
the king or the sultan dies before the messengers return,
those messengers become prisoners or slaves to whichever side they belong, whether Christians or Saracens.

While this misfortune overtook our people who were
on land, the same thing happened to us who were on
the water; for the wind blew from Damietta, and coun-
teracted the current, and the knights whom the king
had placed in his light vessels to defend the sick fled

away. Our sailors, too, left the main stream and got into a creek, so that we were obliged to turn back again towards the Saracens.

As we were going along by water, we came, just before the dawn broke, to the passage where were lying the sultan's galleys that had prevented supplies from coming to us from Damietta. A great tumult arose, for they fired against ourselves and against our people who were riding along the bank of the river such a quantity of darts dipped in Greek fire that it seemed as if the stars were falling from the skies.

When our sailors had extricated us from the arm of the river into which we had strayed, we came upon the king's light boats which the king had assigned for the protection of our sick fleeing in all haste to Damietta. Then a wind arose coming from Damietta, which blew so strong as to neutralize the current. On both sides of the river there was a great number of small boats belonging to our people which were unable to make downward way, and had been stopped and captured by the Saracens. And they put the people to death and threw their bodies into the water, and pulled out the chests and baggage from the vessels they had taken. The Saracens who were upon the bank on horseback kept on discharging darts at us because we would not go to them. My people had fastened upon me a tourney hauberk, which I had put on lest some of the darts which fell into our vessel might wound me. At that moment my people who were in the forepart of the vessel called out to me : " Sir, sir, your sailors, because the Saracens are threatening them, mean to take you ashore." I raised myself up by my arms, weak as I was, and drew my sword upon them, and declared that I would slay them if they took me ashore. They replied

that I might choose which I would have done, either
they would take me ashore, or they would anchor in
the middle of the river until the wind went down. I
told them that I would rather they anchored in the
middle of the river than be taken ashore, where I saw
we should be slain, so they let go the anchor.

It was not long before we saw four of the sultan's
galleys approach, with a thousand men on board. Then
I called my knights and my people, and asked what
they desired we should do, whether surrender ourselves
to the Sultan's galleys, or to the people who were on
the bank.

We all agreed that we should prefer surrendering
ourselves to the sultan's galleys, because they would
keep us all together, to surrendering ourselves to those
who were on the land, because they would separate us,
and sell us to the Bedaween. Then one of my clerks,
who was a native of Doullens, said: "Sir, I do not
hold to this council." I asked him to what he would
hold, and he said: "I am of opinion that we should let
ourselves be killed, so shall we all go to Paradise." But
we did not agree with him.

When I saw that we must be taken, I threw a casket,
with my jewels and relics, into the river. Then one of
my sailors said to me: "Sir, if you do not let me say
that you are the king's cousin, they will put us all to
death, and you with us." I told him that I was quite
willing that he should say what he pleased. When the
people in the first galley, who were coming to run us
down amidships, heard that, they cast out their anchors
close to our vessel. Then God sent a Saracen, who was
of the emperor's land, who swam to our vessel, and,
throwing his arms round me, said: "Sir, you are lost
if you do not act with resolution, for you must leap

from your vessel on to the beak of that galley: if you take the leap they will not notice you, for they are thinking of the plunder of your vessel." They threw me a rope from the galley, and I sprang on to the beak, as it pleased God. But I tottered, and had not the Saracen leaped after me, to support me, I should have fallen into the water.

They took me into the galley, where there were at least 280 of their men, and he kept his arm always round me. Then the others threw me down, and jumped upon my body to cut my throat, for whoever killed me would have felt himself honoured. But this Saracen always held me in his arms, and kept calling out, " The king's cousin !" Twice they threw me down, and once upon my knees, and then I felt the knife at my throat. In this ordeal God preserved me by means of this Saracen, who brought me to the tower (on the deck) in which the Saracen knights were assembled. When I came into the midst of them, they took off my hauberk, and, moved by compassion, threw over me a scarlet coverlid, lined with miniver which my lady mother had given me, and one of them brought me a white girdle, with which I girt myself outside my coverlid, in which I had made a hole and had put it on; and another brought me a hood which I put over my head. And then, because of the fear I had, and also because of my illness, I began greatly to tremble. And I asked for something to drink, and they brought me some in a vessel; but as soon as I took it in my mouth to swallow it, it spurted out of my nostrils. When I saw that, I sent for my people, and told them I was a dead man, for I had a gathering in my throat. They asked me how I knew that, and as soon as they saw the water come out of my throat and nostrils, they began to weep.

When the Saracen knights who were there saw my people weeping, they asked the Saracen who had saved our lives why they were weeping. And he replied that he thought I had a gathering in the throat, and therefore it was all over with me. Then one of the Saracen knights told him who had saved us to bid us be of good cheer, for he would give me something to take that would cure me in two days, and he did so.

The grand-admiral of the galleys sent for me, and asked me if I was the king's cousin. And I answered him no; and told him how and why the sailor had said that I was. He replied that I had acted wisely, for otherwise we should all have been dead men. Then he asked me if I was in any way connected with the Emperor Frederick of Germany, who was at that time living. And I answered that I believed my mother was his cousin-german. Upon which he said that he should like me all the better for it. While we were at dinner, he sent for a burgess of Paris; and when the burgess came he said to me: " Sir, what are you doing ?"

" What am I doing then ?" I asked.

" Why, in God's name," exclaimed he, " you are eating meat on Friday ! "

When I heard that, I put my trencher behind me. Then the admiral asked my Saracen why I did that, and he told him. And the admiral observed that God would not be angered with me for what I had done, as I did not do it wittingly. And that is the very answer the legate made me when we were out of captivity. But for all that I have not since omitted to fast on bread and water every Friday in Lent, on which account the legate was very angry with me, because there remained near the king no other rich man than myself. The Sunday afterwards the admiral ordered myself, and all the other prisoners who had been taken upon the water, to be landed on the bank. While they were dragging Monseigneur John, my good priest, out of the hold of the galley, he fainted, whereupon they killed him, and threw him into the river. His clerk, who also fainted through the army sickness which was upon him, had a cap clapped upon his head; but he, too, was slain, and flung into the river. While the other invalids were being landed from the galleys in which they had been imprisoned, there were Saracens ready with drawn swords to put to death all who fell, and who were then cast into the river. I said to them, by means of my Saracen, that it seemed to me that they were acting wrongly, because it was contrary to Saladin's instructions, who declared that no one ought to take a man's life after allowing him to partake of his bread and salt. The admiral replied that they were men of no account, for they were unable to hold up against the sickness that was upon them. He ordered my sailors to be brought before me, and said that they had all abjured Christianity. I told him not to place any trust in them, for they would abandon him just as readily as they had abandoned us. The admiral made answer that he agreed with me, for Saladin had said that he never knew a good Saracen become a good Christian, or a good Christian become a good Saracen. After these things, he mounted me upon a palfrey, and made me go by his side. And we crossed a bridge of boats, and went to Mansourah, where the king and his army were prisoners. And we came to the entrance of a large tent, in which were the sultan's scribes, and they made me write my name. Then my Saracen said to me: "Sir, I cannot follow you any further, but I pray you, sir, to hold always by the hand the child you have with you, lest the Saracens should carry him off from you." And this child was named Bartholomew, and was the bastard of the Seigneur de Montfaucon. As soon as my name was written down, the admiral led me to the tent where the barons were and upwards of 10,000 people with them. When I entered, all the barons expressed so much joy, that not a word could be heard; and they gave thanks to our Lord, and said they thought I was lost.

CHAPTER VIII.

WE had not remained there long when one of the richest men who were there made us rise, and conducted us to another tent. The Saracens kept many knights and others prisoners in a court inclosed within walls. From this inclosure in which they were placed, they were taken out one after the other, and asked, "Will you abjure?" Those who refused were placed on one side and beheaded; and those who abjured were placed on the other side. About this time the sultan sent us his council to speak to us, and they demanded to whom they should repeat the sultan's message to us. And we told them to say what they had to say to the good Count Peter of Brittany. There were individuals there who understood both the Saracen and the French tongues, who are called dragomans, and these rendered the Saracen into French for Count Peter. And these were the words they interchanged: "Sir, the Sultan sends us to you to know if you would be set free?"

The count replied, " Yes,"

" And what would you give the sultan for your freedom?"

" Whatever we could reasonably do and endure," answered the count.

" Would you give," they continued, " for your freedom, any of the castles of the barons in the east ?"

The count explained that he had no power over these castles, because they were held of the emperor of Germany, who was then still living. Then they asked if we would surrender for our freedom any of the castles of the Temple or of the Hospital. The count answered that could not be ; for that when governors were placed in them, they were sworn on relics not to give up any one of the castles for any man's deliverance. Whereupon they replied that it seemed to them we had no great desire to be set free, and that they would go and send us some who would make short work of us with the sword, as they had done with the others. Then they went away.

As soon as they were gone, there rushed into our tent a great crowd of young Saracens, with swords girded by their sides, who brought with them a man of great age, and gray haired, who asked us if it were true that we believed in a God who had been taken, and wounded, and put to death for our sakes, and on the third day brought to life again.

We answered, " Yes."

Then he told us we ought not to be disheartened if we had suffered these persecutions for Him ; " for," said he, " you have not yet died for Him as He died for you, and, if He had power to raise Himself from the dead, be assured He will deliver you when it pleases Him."

Then he went away, and all the young men with him, whereat I was well content, for I certainly thought that they had come to cut off our heads. Not much time elapsed after that before the sultan's people came and told us that the king had procured our deliverance.

After the old man had gone away who had bade us be of good cheer, the sultan's counsellors came to us and said that the king had effected our deliverance, and that we were to send to him four of our people to hear what he had done. We sent to him Monseigneur John de Valery, the worthy man, Monseigneur Philip de Montfort, Monseigneur Baldwin d'Ibelin, seneschal of Cyprus, and Monseigneur Guy d'Ibelin, constable of Cyprus, one of the most accomplished knights I have ever seen, and who greatly loved the people of that country. These four seigneurs brought us back word in what manner the king had obtained our deliverance, and it was in this wise.

The sultan's counsellors tempted the king in the same manner that they had tried us, to see if the king would promise to deliver to them any of the castles of the Temple or the Hospital, or of the barons of the country; and, as it pleased God, the king replied exactly as we had replied. Then they threatened him, and told him that if he would not do that they would put him into the *bernicles*. The *bernicles* are the most cruel torture that any one can be subjected to. They consist of two pieces of flexible wood, indented at the end, which dovetail into one another, and they are bound together at the end with strong straps of ox-hide. And when they mean to put people into them, they lay them on their side, and place their legs between the teeth, and then they make a man sit down upon the pieces of wood, in consequence of which there will not remain six inches of bone anywhere that is not crushed. To do the worst they can, at the end of three days, when the legs are swollen, they again place them in the berniclos, and crush them afresh. To these threats the king replied that he was their prisoner, and they could do to him what they pleased.

When they saw that they could not move the good king by menaces, they returned to him and asked how much money he would give the sultan, besides delivering to him Damietta. He replied that if the sultan would accept a reasonable sum of money, he would ask the queen to pay it for their deliverance.

They said, "Why will you not say that you will do these things?"

The king made answer that he could not tell if the queen would do it, because she was his liege-lady. Thereupon the counsellors went back to speak to the sultan, and they brought back word to the king, that if. the queen would pay a million gold bezants, which were equivalent to 500,000 *livres*, he would set the king free. The king asked them, upon their oath, if the sultan would let them go for that sum, provided the queen consented. So they returned to the sultan, and when they came back again they took an oath to the king that they would free him on those terms. As soon as they had sworn, the king promised the emirs that he would willingly pay 500,000 *livres* for the liberation of his people, and would surrender Damietta for his own freedom; for that he was not of a condition to be ransomed for money. When the sultan heard that, he said: "By my faith, this Frank is open-handed not to have bargained about so large a sum of money. Go and tell him," added the sultan, "that I present him with a hundred thousand *livres* to pay the ransom."

Then the sultan had the men of importance placed in four galleys to be conveyed to Damietta. In the galley in which I was placed were the good Count Peter of

Brittany, the Count William of Flanders, the good
Count John of Soissons, Monseigneur Imbert de Beaujeu, constable of France, the good knight Monseigneur
John d'Ibelin, and Monseigneur Guy, his brother.
Those who commanded the galley lay to in front of an
encampment which the sultan had formed upon the
bank of the river after the following fashion.   In front
of the camp there was a tower constructed of fir-poles,
and closed round with coloured calico : this was the
entrance to the encampment.   Within this entrance a
tent was pitched in which the emirs when they were
going to speak to the sultan left their swords and weapons.   Behind this tent there was a doorway similar
to the first, by which you entered a large tent, which
.was the sultan's hall.   Behind the hall there was a tower
like the one in front, through which you entered the
sultan's chamber.   Behind the sultan's chamber there
was an enclosed space, and in the centre of this
enclosure a tower loftier than all the others, from
which the sultan looked out over the whole camp and
country.   From the enclosure a pathway went down to
the river to a spot where the sultan had spread a tent
over the water for the purpose of bathing.   The whole
of this encampment was enclosed within a trellis of
woodwork, and on the outer side the trellises were spread
with blue calico, so that those who were outside might
not look within ; and the four towers were also covered
with calico.

We arrived on Thursday before Ascension-day at
the place where this encampment was spread. The four
galleys in which we were confined were anchored in
front of the sultan's tent.   The king was placed in a
tent not far from the sultan's encampment.   The sultan
had so arranged that on the Saturday before Ascension-

day Damietta was to be given up to him, and he was to
set free the king.

The emirs whom the sultan had dismissed from his
council, and superseded by his own friends whom he
had brought with him from foreign lands, took counsel
among themselves, and one of them, a man of much
shrewdness, spoke to the following effect :—

"Sirs, you see the shame and dishonour the sultan
has wrought us in depriving us of the posts which his
father had confided to us. We may therefore be certain that as soon as he finds himself in the fortress of
Damietta, he will have us seized and leave us to die in
prison, as his grandfather did to the emirs who took prisoners the Count of Bar and the Count of Montfort.
For which reason it seems to me that it is safer for us
to put him to death before he escapes out of our hands."

They went to the men of the Halca, and persuaded
them to slay the sultan immediately after they had eaten
with the sultan, who had invited them as his guests.
And it came to pass that as soon as they had eaten, and
the sultan was proceeding to his chamber, and had taken
leave of his emirs, one of the knights of the Halca who
bore the sultan's sword smote him with his own sword
on the middle of his hand, between the four fingers, and
cleaved it to the wrist. Thereupon the sultan turned
back to his emirs, who were the cause of that being
done to him, and exclaimed :—

"Sirs, I appeal to you against these men of the
Halca, who seek to slay me, as you may see."

Then the knights of the Halca replied with one voice
to the sultan :—

"Sire, thou sayest that we seek to slay thee. It is
better that we should put thee to death than that thou
shouldst kill us "

Then they sounded the cymbals, and all the army came to inquire what was the sultan's pleasure. They answered that Damietta was taken, and that the sultan was on his way thither, and that his orders were that they should follow him. Then all armed themselves, and spurred on towards Damietta. When we saw that they were going towards Damietta, we were seized with a sore heartache, because we believed that Damietta was lost. The sultan, who was young and active, fled to the tower he had built, with three of his imans who sat at meat with him; and this tower was behind his chamber, as you have already heard. Those of the Halca, who were 500 mounted men, levelled the sultan's tents, and surrounded the tower to which he had fled with the three imans, and called to him to come down. Then he said he would do so provided they spared his life. They replied that they would force him to come down, and that he was not in Damietta. So they discharged Greek fire, which caught the tower that was made of fir-poles and calico. The tower burnt rapidly, so that I never beheld a fire so bright and straight. When the sultan saw that, he hurried down, and fled towards the river by the path which I mentioned above. Those of the Halca had broken up the pathway with their swords, and as the sultan hastened along towards the river, one of them smote him between the ribs with a lance, and the sultan fled on, dragging the lance after him. They plunged in after him, swimming, and came and slew him close to the galley where we were. One of the knights, whose name was Faress Eddin Octay, cut him in twain with his sword and tore out his heart. Then he went to the king, with his hand all covered with blood, and said to him: " What wilt thou give to me who have slain thy enemy, who would have made thee die, had he lived?" But the king answered him never a word.

Fully thirty of them came to our galley, brandishing naked swords and Danish battle-axes. I asked Monseigneur Baldwin d'Ibelin, who understood Saracen, what these people were saying; and he replied that they said they had come to cut off our heads. There were a number of us confessing themselves to a friar of La Trinité, who was with Count William of Flanders. But, for my part, I could not recall to mind any sin I had committed, but was thinking that much as I might wish to defend myself, or hide myself away, it would be all the worse for me to attempt it. Then I crossed myself, and knelt down at the feet of one of those who carried a Danish battle-axe, and I said: "Thus died St. Agnes." Messire Guy d'Ibelin, Constable of Cyprus, knelt down by my side and confessed himself to me; and I said to him: "I absolve you, with such power as God has given me." But when I rose from there, I could not remember a single thing he had said or recounted to me.

They removed us from where we were and confined us in the hold of the vessel; and many of our people thought they did it because they did not care to attack us when all together, but would slay us one after the other. Down there we were in a state of cruel suffering in the evening and all night, for we lay so pressed together that my feet were against the face of the good Count Peter of Brittany, while his feet touched my face. On the morrow, the emirs took us out of the prison we were in, and their messengers said that we were to go and confer with them about renewing the convention the sultan had made with us, and they told us to be assured that if the sultan had lived he would have cut off the king's head and ours likewise. Accordingly, those

H

who were able to go went; the Count of Brittany, the constable, and myself, who were grievously ill, remained behind. The Count of Flanders, Count John of Soissons, the two brothers D'Ibelin, and the others went, who were able to stand.

They came to terms with the emirs, who promised that as soon as Damietta was surrendered to them they would set at liberty the king and the other rich men who were there, for as for the common folk, the sultan had sent them back towards Babylon, excepting those he had put to death. And this he had done contrary to the convention he had made with the king, which makes it probable that he would have put us also to death as soon as he recovered Damietta. The king was likewise to swear that he would satisfy them to the amount of 200,000 livres before he got clear of the river, and would send 200,000 from Acre. The Saracens, in conformity with the convention they had made with the king, were to take care of the sick who were at Damietta, the cross-bowmen, the armourers, and the salt provisions, until such time as the king could send for them.

The oaths which the emirs were to take to the king were put down in writing, and were to the following effect :—That if they did not fulfil their agreement they wished they might be dishonoured as one who should go in pilgrimage to Mohammed at Mecca with his head uncovered; and as dishonoured as those who put away their wives and took them back again afterwards. With regard to this second clause, no man can put away his wife, according to the law of Mohammed, without renouncing all idea of ever having her again, unless he sees another man lying with her before he takes her back. Their third oath was after this manner: that if they did not fulfil their agreement, they wished they might be dishonoured as the Saracen who eats pork. The king accepted the oaths of the emirs, because Master Nicholas of Acre, who understood Saracen, affirmed that they could not make any that would be stronger in the eye of their law.

When the emirs had been sworn, they put down in writing the oath they desired the king to take; and it was done according to the advice of certain priests who had renounced their faith; and the writing said that if the king did not fulfil his agreement with the emirs, he was willing to be held in as much dishonour as the Christian who denies God and His mother, and who separates from the company of His twelve Apostles, and of the saints, male and female. To that the king readily consented. The last clause of the oath was this:—that if he did not fulfil his agreement with the emirs, he was willing to be dishonoured like the Christian who denies God and His law, and who, in scorn of God, spits upon the cross and tramples it under foot. When the king heard that, he said: "Please God, I will not take that oath." The emirs sent to the king Master Nicholas, who understood Saracen, and who thus spoke to the king: "Sire, the emirs are much offended that, after they have sworn all you required of them, you refuse to swear what they require of you; and be assured that if you do not take this oath, they will cut off your own head and those of all your people."

The king replied that they could do what they pleased, for he would rather die a good Christian than live hated by God and His mother.

The Patriarch of Jerusalem, an aged and venerable man of eighty years, had obtained a safe-conduct from the Saracens, and had come to the king to help him in negotiating his liberation. Now, it is the custom be-

tween Christians and Saracens that when the king or
sultan dies, the bearers of any messages, whether to
infidels or Christians, become prisoners and slaves ; and
because the sultan who gave him the safe-conduct was
dead, the patriarch had become a prisoner like ourselves. When the king had returned his answer, one of
the emirs declared that it was the patriarch who had
given him this counsel, and he said to the paynim :—

"If you take my advice, I will force the king to
swear, for I will make the patriarch's head fly off into
his lap."

They did not listen to him, however, but seized the
patriarch and dragged him away from the king's side,
and bound him to a tent-pole with his hands behind his
back, and so tightly that his hands became swollen as
large as his head, and the blood started out from his
finger-nails. The patriarch cried out to the king :—

" Sire, swear what they require, for I take upon my
own soul the sin of the oath you make, since you mean
to keep it."

I do not know how this oath was arranged, but the
emirs were satisfied with regard to the oaths of the king
and of the other rich men who were there.

Immediately after the sultan was murdered, his instruments were brought before the king's tent, and he
was told that the emirs had seriously deliberated about
making him Sultan of Babylon. He asked me if I
thought he would have accepted the kingdom of Babylon, supposing it had been offered to him. I said that he
would have acted very foolishly if he had done so, seeing
that they had murdered their lord ; but he replied that, in
good sooth, he would not have refused it. The matter
rested there, because they said the king was the most
steadfast Christian they had ever met with. And they

gave this as an instance, that when he went out from his tent, he prostrated himself crosswise on the ground, and made the sign of the cross himself over his whole person. And they said that if Mohammed had suffered so much evil to befall themselves, they would never have believed in him; and they added that if the Saracens made the king their sultan he would put them all to death, or they would have to become Christians.

When the convention between the king and the emirs. had been concluded and confirmed by oath, it was agreed that they should set us free on the day after Ascension-day; and that as soon as Damietta was restored to the emirs, the king and the rich men who were with him should be released. On Thursday evening, those who conducted our four galleys anchored them in the middle of the river, opposite the bridge of Damietta, and pitched a tent by the bridge, where the king was landed.

At sunrise Monseigneur Geoffrey de Sargines went into the town, and delivered it over to the emirs, who hoisted on the towers of the town the sultan's flag. The Saracen knights rushed into the town, and began to drink the wine, and were soon intoxicated; after which one of them came to our galley, and drew his sword all stained with blood, and said that for his part he had killed six of our people. Before Damietta was delivered up, the queen embarked on board our ships, with all our people who were in the town, excepting the sick. Of these the Saracens were to take care in virtue of their oath, but they murdered all of them. The king's engines, of which likewise they were to take care, they chopped to pieces; nor did they keep the salt pork, a thing they never eat, but they made a heap of the salted meat, and another of the dead bodies, and lighted a fire beneath them, and it was so great a fire that it lasted all Friday, Saturday, and Sunday.

CHAPTER IX.

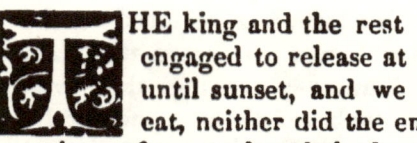

HE king and the rest of us whom they had engaged to release at sunrise were detained until sunset, and we had nothing at all to eat, neither did the emirs eat anything, but were in conference the whole day. An emir said in the name of those who were of his party: " Sirs, if you will listen to me and to those who are of my way of thinking, we will put to death the king and the rich men who are with him, because for the next forty years we risk nothing, for their children are infants, and Damietta is in our hands, wherefore we can do it with all the greater safety." Another Saracen, named Sebreci, a native of Mauritania, spoke against this, and said: " If we kill the king, after slaying the sultan, it will be said that the Egyptians are the most wicked and disloyal people in the world." Then he who proposed that we should be put to death said in reply: "It is very true that we acted very wickedly in killing our sultan, for we went against the commandment of Mohammed, who commanded us to guard our lord as the apple of our eye; and that commandment is written in this book. Now listen," continued he, " to another of Mohammed's commandments which comes directly after it." He turned a page of the book he held in his hand, and showed them the other commandment of Mohammed, which was in this wise: "For the security of the faith, slay the enemy of the law." "Now, see how much we have done amiss contrary to Mohammed's commandments, in that we have slain our lord, and we shall do still worse if we do not slay the king, no matter what sureties we have given him, for he is the most bitter enemy of our law that can be."

Our death was almost decided, whence it happened that an emir who was our enemy, believing that we were all going to be put to death, came down to the river and began to shout out in the Saracen's language to the people who managed the galleys, and taking off his turban made signs to them with it. Straightway they raised the anchor, and took us back a good league towards Babylon. Then we thought we were all lost, and many tears were shed.

But, as it pleased God, who never forgets his servants, it was resolved towards sunset that we should be released. Then they brought us back, and drew our galleys close to the bank. We asked them to let us go, but they said they would not do so until we had eaten something, "for that it would be a disgrace to the emirs if you were to depart from our prisons fasting." And we told them to give us some food, and we would eat of it ; and they answered that it had been sent for to the camp. The provisions they brought us were cheese fritters, toasted in the sun so that worms should not breed in them, and hard boiled eggs cooked four or five days before ; and to do us honour they had painted them outside of various colours.

They put us on shore, and we went towards the king, whom they were conducting towards the river from the

tent in which they had confined him ; and there followed
him on foot fully 20,000 Saracens with swords girded
on their sides.   In the river, right before the king, lay a
Genevese galley, in which there appeared only a single
man upon the deck.   As soon as he perceived the king
on the river's bank he gave a whistle, and in an instant
there sprang out of the hold eighty cross-bowmen all
armed, with their crossbows set, into which they quickly
fitted their bolts.   As soon as the Saracens saw that,
they ran away like so many sheep, so that none remained with the king save only two or three.   A plank
was thrown to the land for the king to cross upon, and
for the Count of Anjou, his brother, Monseigneur Geoffrey de Sargines, Monseigneur Philip de Nemours, the
Marshal of France, named Du Mez, the Superior of the
Mathurins, and myself.   As for the Count of Poitiers,
he was detained in prison until the king had paid the
200,000 livres which he was bound to pay before leaving
the river.

The Saturday after Ascension-day, the day after that
on which we were released, there came to take leave of
the king, the Count of Flanders, the Count of Soissons,
and many other rich men who had been prisoners in the
galleys.   The king said to them that he thought they
would do well to wait until the Count of Poitiers, his
brother, was set free.   But they replied that it was not
in their power, as the galleys were ready to go to sea.
So they embarked on board, taking with them the good
Count Peter of Brittany, who was so ill that he survived
only three weeks, and died at sea.

The operation of paying began on Saturday morning,
and occupied the whole of Saturday, and all Sunday
until nightfall ; the payment was made by the balance,
each weighing being worth 10,000 livres.   When Sun-

day evening arrived, the king's people who were effecting the payment informed the king that they were
30,000 livres short.   There were then with the king
only the King of Sicily, the Marshal of France, the Superior of the Mathurins, and myself; all the others being
busy about the payment.   Thereupon I said to the king
that it would be well to send for the commander and the
marshal of the Temple (for the master was dead), and
require of them to lend him 30,000 livres to deliver his
brother.   The king sent for them, and commanded me
to tell them.   When I had done so, brother Stephen
d'Odricourt, the commander of the Temple, spoke to me
thus :—

" Sire de Joinville, the counsel which you give is
neither good nor reasonable ; for you know that the de-
posits we receive we are bound by our oaths not to give
up to any but to those who have confided them to us."

Many harsh and insulting words passed between us ;
and then brother Reginald de Vichiers, who was Marshal of the Temple, took up the word, and said : " Sire,
pay no heed to the dispute between the Seigneur de
Joinville and our commander ; for, as our commander
observes, we cannot give up anything without being
perjured ; and as to what the seneschal counsels you,
that if we will not lend it you should take it, there is
nothing very wonderful in that, and you can do as you
please ; if you take of ours, we have enough of yours
in Acre to indemnify ourselves."

I said to the king that I was ready to go, if such was
his pleasure, and he commanded me to do so.   I proceeded towards one of the galleys of the Temple, the
chief galley, and when I was about to descend into the hold
where the treasure was kept, I begged the commander
of the Temple to come and see how much I took ; but

he did not deign to come. The marshal said he would come to witness what violence I used. As soon as I had got down to where the treasure was, I asked the treasurer of the Temple to hand me the keys of a chest that was in front of me; but he, seeing me lean and gaunt with illness, and in the dress I wore in captivity, refused to give them to me. Perceiving a hatchet lying on the ground, I picked it up, and said that I would turn it into the king's key. When the marshal saw that, he caught me by the wrist and said: " Sir, we see that you mean to use violence, and will compel us to give up the keys." Then he commanded the treasurer to give them to me; and when the marshal told the treasurer who I was, he was all amazed. I found that the chest I opened belonged to Nicholas de Choisi, one of the king's sergeants. I threw out what money I found in it, and they let me carry it to the prow of the vessel that had brought me; and I took the Marshal of France and left him with the money; and on the galley I placed the Superior of the Mathurins. The marshal handed the money to the superior, and he handed it to me in the vessel where I was. When we approached the king's galley, I called out to the king: " Sire, Sire, see how I am supplied." And the holy man saw me gladly and with joy. We handed over to those who were effecting the payment the money I had brought.

When the payment was completed, the king's counsellors who had managed it came to him, and said that the Saracens refused to release his brother until they had got the money into their own possession. Some of the council were of opinion that the king should not give up the money until he had got his brother back. But the king replied that he would pay it over to them, because he had promised it to them, and, for their

part, they would fulfil what they had promised him,
if they intended to do what was right. Monseigneur
Philip de Nemours then told the king that an error of
10,000 livres had been made to the prejudice of the
Saracens. And the king was much angered, and said
that he desired that the 10,000 livres should be made
good to them, for he had promised to pay the 200,000
livres before he left the river. Upon that I touched
Monseigneur Philip with my foot, and bade the king
not to believe him, because he was saying what was not
true, for the Saracens were the greatest cheats in the
world. And Monseigneur Philip said that I spoke the
truth, for what he had said was in jest. The king
remarked that such jesting was misplaced. "And I
command you," said he to Monseigneur Philip, "by the
fealty you owe me as my vassal, that, if the 10,000 livres
have not been paid, you will see that they are paid."

Many persons had urged the king to go on board his
own ship, which awaited him off the shore, to withdraw
himself beyond the power of the Saracens. Never
would the king listen to anyone on that point, but
always answered that he would not leave the river
until he had paid them the 200,000 livres, according to
his promise. As soon as the payment was effected, the
king, without any one asking him, said that his oath
was now discharged, and that we might proceed to his
ship, which was lying off the shore. Then our galley
was set in motion, and we went a good league before
any one spoke to his neighbour, because of the anxiety
we felt for the Count of Poitiers. At that moment
Monseigneur Philip de Montfort came up to us in a
galliot, and cried to the king: "Sire, Sire, speak to
your brother, the Count of Poitiers, who is in that
other ship." Thereupon the king exclaimed: "Light

up! Light up!" And so it was done. Then there was as much joy among us as there could be.

The king embarked on board his ship, and we with him. A poor fisherman went to tell the Countess of Poitiers that he had seen the Count of Poitiers set at liberty, and she ordered twenty livres parisis to be given to him.

I must not omit certain things that happened in Egypt while we were there. First of all I will tell you of Monseigneur Walter de Châtillon, which a knight, whose name was Monseigneur John de Monson, related to me. He said he saw Monseigneur de Châtillon, in a street that was in the village where the king was made prisoner, and this street passed right through the village, so that you saw the fields from both ends. In this street Monseigneur Walter de Châtillon posted himself, with his naked sword in his hand. When he saw the Turks come into this street, he rushed at them, sword in hand, and chaced them out of the village; but while fleeing before him, the Turks, who fired as well from behind as from the front, covered him with darts. When he had driven them out of the village, he pulled out the darts that stuck in him, again adjusted his armour, raised himself up in his stirrups, stretched out his arm with the sword, and cried aloud: "Châtillon, knight! where are my men of valour?" Turning round, he saw the Turks had entered by the other end, and charged them afresh, sword in hand; and this he did three times, in the manner above described. When the admiral of the galleys took me to those who had been made prisoners on land, I inquired about him of those who were in his company; but I could not find anyone to tell me how he was taken, except Monseigneur John Frumons, the good knight, who said that when they brought him to Mansourah, he encountered a Turk mounted upon Monseigneur Walter Châtillon's war-horse, and the crupper was covered with blood. And he asked what he had done with him to whom the horse belonged, and the Turk replied that he had cut his throat upon his own horse, as appeared from the stains of blood upon the crupper. •

There was in the army a very valiant man, whose name was Monseigneur James de Castel, bishop of Soissons. When he saw that our people were retracing their steps to Damietta, he had so great a desire to go to God, that he would not return to the country in which he was born. So he was all in a haste to go to God, and, spurring forward, attacked the Turks single-handed, who, with their sword-cuts, slew him, and placed him in the presence of God, in the army of martyrs. While the king was waiting for the completion of the payment which his people were making to the Turks for the liberation of his brother, the Count of Poitiers, a Saracen, handsomely attired, and of good mien, came to the king, and presented to him curdled milk[1] in jars, and flowers of different kinds, on the part of the children of the *nazac* of the former sultan of Babylon; and in presenting them he spoke French. The king asked him where he had learnt French, and the man answered that he had been a Christian. Whereupon the king exclaimed : "Begone! I will not speak another word to you." I took him aside, and asked what was his condition. He told me that he was born at Provins, and that he came into Egypt with King John, and that he had married in Egypt, and was a great lord.

---

[1] Probably clarified butter, like the Indian *ghee*.

Then I said to him : "Are you ignorant that if you die in this state you will go to hell?"

And he answered: "Yes (for he was certain that there was no religion so good as the Christian religion), but I fear, if I return to you, the poverty and the reproaches I should suffer. They would be always crying after me: 'There's the·renegade!' So I prefer to live with riches and in peace, rather than reduce myself to such a position as I foresee."

I told him that at the day of judgment, when every-one would see his sin, he would have to endure far worse reproaches than those he spoke about. And many more good words I said to him, which had no effect. In this frame of mind he quitted me, and I saw no more of him.

You have heard in the preceding pages of the sore persecutions which the king and we had to endure; from similar miseries the queen herself did not escape, as you shall now learn. Three days before she was confined, the news reached her that the king was a prisoner, at which tidings she was so terrified that, whenever she fell asleep in her bed, it seemed to her that her room was full of Saracens, and she screamed, "Help! help!" And for fear that the child with which she was big should perish, she made an old knight, eighty years of age, lie down in front of her bed, and hold her by the hand. Every time the queen called out he would say : "Madam, be not afraid, I am here." Before she was delivered, she ordered everyone out of her chamber, except this knight, at whose feet she knelt, and demanded of him a boon; and the knight plighted his oath.

And she said to him : "I require of you, by the faith you have pledged to me, that if the Saracens capture this city, you will cut off my head, rather than that they shall take me."

And the knight made answer: " Be assured that I will do so without fail, for I had already resolved to kill you before they should have made prisoners of us."

The queen was delivered of a son, who was named John, and they called him Tristan, because of the great sorrow in which he was born. The very day on which she was confined, she was told that they of Pisa and Genoa, and the other cities, proposed to take to flight.

On the morrow after her confinement she summoned them all to her bedside, so that the chamber was full of them: " Sirs, for God's sake do not leave this town, for you know that monseigneur, the king, will be lost with all who are with him, should it be taken. And if that does not move you, at least take pity upon this poor creature lying here, and wait until I can rise from my couch."

And they answered, " Madam, how can we do so? We are perishing of hunger in this town."

Then she told them they should not go away because of famine, " for I will buy up all the provisions in the town, and from this moment I retain you in the king's service."

They consulted together, and when they came back to her, they promised that they would remain ungrudgingly, and the queen (whom may God absolve!) bought up all the provisions in the town, which cost her 360,000 livres. Besides all this, she was obliged to get up before her time, because of the place being restored to the Saracens. So she went away to Acre, to await the king.

While the king was waiting for his brother's release,

he sent brother Raoul, a Dominican friar, to an emir, whose name was Faress-Eddin-Octay, one of the most loyal Saracens I ever met. He told him that he was astonished how he and the other emirs could suffer the treaty to be so villainously violated; for they had murdered his sick, of whom they were pledged to take care, and destroyed his engines, and burnt his sick and his salted pork, which also they ought to have preserved. Faress-Eddin-Octay replied to brother Raoul, and said, "Brother Raoul, tell the king that, because of my law, I cannot remedy the matter, and that weighs upon my mind. And tell him, too, from me, that he must not let it appear that he is pained at this, so long as he is in our hands, or he is a dead man." His opinion was, that until the king reached Acre, he should give no thought to it.

When the king got on board his ship, he found that his people had made no preparations for him, neither bed, nor clothing; but, until he reached Acre, he was obliged to lie on the bedding which the sultan had given him. And he put on the robe which the sultan had had made for him, of black samit, lined with fur of various colours, and minever, and ornamented with a great quantity of gold buttons.

For six days, while we were at sea, I, who was sick, was always seated by the king's side. Then he recounted to me how he was taken, and how, with God's help, he had effected our ransom and his own. And he made me tell him how I was taken upon the water; and afterwards he said that I ought to be very thankful to our Lord that He had delivered me out of such great perils. He regretted bitterly the death of the Count of Artois, his brother, and said that he had been prevented, much against his will, from coming to see him, as did the Count of Poitiers, and that nothing else would have kept him from coming to see him on board his galleys.

He also complained to me of his brother, the Count of Anjou, who was in the same ship, but never bore him company. One day he asked what the Count of Anjou was doing, and was told that he was playing at back-gammon with Monseigneur Walter de Nemours. He went to the spot, tottering from the weakness caused by his illness, and, seizing the dice and the boards, flung them into the sea, and was very wrathful with his brother because he had so soon taken to playing with dice. Monseigneur Walter came off the best, for he swept into his lap all the money that was on the board, and there was a considerable amount, with which he walked off.

CHAPTER X.

WHEN the king reached Acre, all the processions came down to the sea-shore to meet and receive him, with great demonstrations of joy. A palfrey was brought for me. As soon as I had mounted it, I turned faint, and told him who brought the palfrey to hold me for fear I should tumble off. With great difficulty I was helped up the steps of the king's palace. I seated myself at a window, and a child came and sat beside me, about ten years of age, named Bartholomew, the bastard son of Monseigneur Ami de Montbéliard, Seigneur de Montfaucon. While I was sitting there, and no one attending to me, there came up to me a valet, in a red coat with two yellow stripes, who bowed to me, and asked if I remembered him. And I said, No. Then he told me he was from Oiselay, my uncle's château. I asked him to whom he belonged. And he answered, to no one, but that he would stay with me if I pleased. And I told him that I should be much pleased. He immediately went to procure some white coifs for me, and combed my hair carefully. The king then sent for me to eat with him, and I went in the vest that had been made for me in prison, out of the clippings of my cloak; and I made

over to the child Bartholomew my cloak and four ells
of camelot, which had been given to me in prison for
the love of God. Guillemin, my new valet, carved before me, and procured food for the child, while we were
at table.

My new squire told me that he had found me a
lodging near the baths, where I could be cleansed from
all the filth I had brought with me out of prison. In
the evening, while I was in the bath, my heart failed
me, and I fainted, and with much difficulty I was taken
out of the bath to my bed. On the morrow an old
knight, named Monseigneur Peter de Bourbonne, came
to see me, and I took him into my service. He became
bail for me in the town for what I wanted in the way
of dress and equipment. When I had got myself into
order, fully four days after our arrival, I went to see
the king, who scolded me, and said that I had not done
well in delaying so long to come and see him, and he
commanded me, as I valued his love, to eat at his table
every day, morning and evening, until such time as he
had decided what we should do, whether return to France,
or stay where we were. I told the king that Monseigneur
Peter de Courtenay owed me 400 *livres* of my pay,
which he refused to pay me. The king replied that he
would take care I should be paid out of the money
which he himself owed to the Seigneur de Courtenay,
and this he did by the advice of Monseigneur Peter de
Bourbonne. We took 40 *livres* for our expenses, and
the rest we entrusted to the keeping of the commander
of the palace of the Temple. When I had spent the 40
livres, I sent father John Caym de Sainte-Menehould,
whom I had engaged in that foreign land, to bring me
other 40 *livres* The commander replied that he had no
money of mine, and that he knew nothing of me. I

went to brother Reginald de Vichiers, who had become master of the Temple through the king's influence, on account of the courtesy which I mentioned he had shown us in the time of our captivity, and I complained to him of the commander of the palace, who refused to restore to me the money which I had confided to him. When he heard that, he flew into a passion, and said: "Sire de Joinville, I like you much; but be assured that if you do not desist from this demand I shall not like you any more, for you would have people believe that our brethren are thieves." I told him that I should not desist, if it pleased God. For four days I was in this perplexity, as one who had no money left to spend. But at the end of the four days, the master came to me, laughing, and said that he had found my money. The way in which it was found was this; he had changed the commander of the palace, and had sent him to a town called Sephouri, and he restored me my money.

The bishop of Acre of that day, who was a native of Provins, lent to me the house of the priest of St. Michael's. I had engaged Caym de Sainte-Memehould, who served me faithfully for two years, better than any one I had ever had in my service. Now it chanced that there was at the head of my bed a closet through which was an entrance into the church. And it came to pass that a non-intermittent fever seized me, which confined me to my bed, and all my people were in the same strait; for not a single day all that time had I any one to help me to rise; and I looked only for death, because of a warning that was at my ear; for there was not a day in which twenty dead bodies or more were not brought to the church; and from my bed, every time they were carried in, I heard chanted, *Libera me, Domine*. Then I wept, and returned thanks to God, and said :—

" Sire, praised be Thou for this affliction Thou sendest upon me, for I have shown much pride in my dress and carriage ; and I beseech Thee, Sire, to help me, and to deliver out of this illness myself and my people."

After all this I asked my new valet, Guillemin, for his account ; and I found that he had wronged me of upwards of ten *livres tournois*. And when I demanded them of him he said he would repay me as soon as he had the means to do so. I gave him his dismissal, and told him that I made him a present of what he owed me ; for he had well earned it. I learnt from some Burgundian knights, that when they returned from captivity they had brought him with them in their company, and that he was the most obliging thief in the world—for if a knight wanted a knife or belt, gauntlets or spurs, he would steal it and then present it to him.

During the time the king was at Acre his brothers amused themselves by dice-playing ; and the Count of Poitiers played so generously that when he was a winner he would throw open his hall and call for the gentlemen and ladies, if there were any there, and distribute by handfuls both his own money and that which he had won. And when he was a loser, he bought up by valuation the money of those with whom he had played, whether his brother the Count of Anjou or others : and he gave away everything, both what belonged to himself, and what belonged to others.

While we were at Acre the king one Sunday summoned together his brothers and the Count of Flanders, and the other men of quality, and spoke to them after this manner :—

" Sirs, the queen, my mother, has urged and prayed me, all she could, to go back to France ; for my kingdom is in great peril ; for I have neither peace nor truce with the king of England. Those of this country, to whom I have spoken on the subject, say that if I go away this country is lost—for those who are in Acre will all follow after me, because no one will dare to remain with so few people. Therefore, I entreat you," said he, " to think it over; and, as it is a serious business, I give you a week from this day to make me such a reply as seems good to you."

The legate told me that he did not see how the king could stay; and he begged me very earnestly to return in the same ship with himself. But I replied that I could not do so, because, as he was aware, I had nothing left—having lost all when I was taken prisoner in the river. I made this reply to him, though I should have been very glad to have gone with him, because of a counsel given to me when I was setting out by Monseigneur de Boulaincourt, my cousin-german, (whom may God absolve !)—

" You are going away over the sea," said he; " take care how you come back—for no knight, whether rich or poor, can return without shame if he leave in the hands of the Saracens the humble servants of our Lord, in whose company he set out." The legate was angry with me, and said that I ought not to have refused him.

On the following Sunday we again came before the king, who demanded of his brothers and the other barons, and the Count of Flanders, what counsel they were agreed to give him, whether to go away or to stay. They all replied that they had charged Monseigneur Guy de Mauvoisin to give utterance to the advice they wished to offer to the king. The king commanded him to repeat what they had instructed him to say; and he spoke to this effect :—

" Sire, your brothers and the men of quality who are

here, have considered your state, and see that you cannot remain in this country with honour to yourself and
your kingdom ; for of all the knights who came in your
company, and of whom you brought to Cyprus 2900,
there are not in this town a hundred survivors. Therefore, sire, they advise that you should return to France,
and collect troops and money, with which you can
speedily come back to this country to avenge yourself
upon the enemies of God who kept you in prison."

The king was unwilling to rest content with what
Monseigneur Guy de Mauvoisin had said, so he questioned the Count of Anjou, the Count of Poitiers, the
Count of Flanders, and many other men of quality who
were sitting near them, and all agreed with Monseigneur
Guy de Mauvoisin. The legate asked Count John of
Jaffa, who was seated next to these, what he thought of
all this. The count begged him to abstain from such a
question, " because," said he, " my fortresses are on the
frontier, and if I counselled the king to remain, it might
be thought that I did so for my own advantage." Then
the king insisted upon his saying what he thought. And
the count replied that, " if he could contrive to carry
on the campaign for one year, he would gain much
honour by remaining."

Then the legate questioned all who were seated next
below the Count of Jaffa, and all agreed with Monseigneur Guy de Mauvoisin. I was the fortieth, and sat
opposite the legate. He asked me what I thought about
it, and I replied that I was of the opinion of the Count
of Jaffa.

The legate said to me angrily, " How is it possible
that the king could carry on a campaign with so few
troops as he has ?"

I replied also in an angry tone, because it seemed to

me that he said that to annoy me : " Sir, I will tell you, if you wish it. People, sir, say (I know not if it be true) that the king thus far has spent none of his own money, but only that of the clergy. Let the king, then, spend some of his own money, and send for knights to the Morea, and to the countries beyond sea; and when it is rumoured abroad that the king gives liberally, knights will come to him from all parts, and by that means, if it please God, he will be able to carry on a campaign for a year. And by staying he will compass the deliverance of the poor prisoners who have been taken while serving God and himself, and who will never be released if the king goes away."

There was no one there who had not some friends or relatives in prison ; so that no one replied to me, but all burst into tears. After myself the legate questioned Monseigneur William de Beaumont, who was then Marshal of France, and who said that I had spoken very properly, " and I will tell you why," he added. Monseigneur John de Beaumont, the good knight, his uncle, who had a great longing to return to France, apostrophised him very insultingly, and exclaimed, " Filth that you are ! what do you mean to say ? Sit down and hold your tongue !" The king said to him, " Messire John, you are doing wrong; let him speak." " Assuredly, sire, I will not let him do so." The marshal was obliged to remain in silence, and no one agreed with me save the Sire de Chatenay.

Then the king said to us, " Sirs, I have heard all you have to say, and will let you know what it is my pleasure to do, in a week from this day."

When we had taken our leave then the attack began against me from all sides: " The king must be mad, Sire de Joinville, if he does not listen to you in pre-

ference to the whole council of the kingdom of France."
When the tables were set out the king made me sit next
to him during the meal, in the place where he usually
made me sit when his brothers were not there. He
spoke to me never a word while the meal lasted, which
was contrary to his usual custom; for he never failed
to pay attention to me while eating. And I really
thought that he was angry with me, because I had said
that he had not yet spent any of his own money; whereas
he had expended it largely. While the king was listening to the Thanksgiving, I went to a barred window
that was in a recess near the head of the king's bed, and
I passed my arms through the bars; and I was thinking
that if the king went away to France I would go to the
prince of Antioch (with whom I was connected, and
who had sent for me), until such time as another crusade
came into the country, by means of which the prisoners
might be released, according to the advice given to me
by the Sire de Boulaincourt. While I was standing
there the king came and leaned upon my shoulders, and
put his two hands upon my head. I thought it was
Monseigneur Philip de Nemours, who had annoyed me
incessantly all that day because of the counsel I had
given the king, and I said, " Leave me in peace, Monseigneur Philip!" By accident, as I turned my head
round, the king's hand slipped down over my face, and
I saw it was the king by an emerald he wore on his
finger. And he said to me, " Keep still, for I want to
ask you how so young a man as you had the hardihood to
venture to counsel me to stay here, contrary to all the
great and wise men of France who advised me to depart?"

" Sire," said I, " it seemed to my mind an evil thing
that you should return to France, therefore I would not,
for any price, counsel you to do so."

"Do you say," he asked, "that I should act wrongly if I went away?"

"Yes, sire," I answered; "so help me God!"

Then said he: "If I remain, will you remain?"

"Yes, sire, if I can, either at my own charge, or at that of some one else."

"Be at ease, then," he answered, "for I am greatly obliged to you for the counsel you gave; but do not say so to any one all this week."

I was more at my ease after these words, and defended myself more boldly against those who attacked me. Peter d'Avallon accordingly recommended me to defend myself against those who called me "poulain"[1] by saying that I would rather be a poulain than a recreant hack such as they were.

On the next Sunday we came again to the king, and when we were all assembled he made the sign of the cross over his mouth, and spoke to us after this manner (after he had besought the aid of the Holy Ghost, as I suppose, for my mother told me that whenever I wished to say anything I should pray for the aid of the Holy Ghost and cross myself on the mouth). These were the king's words:—

"Sirs, I heartily thank all those who have counselled me to return to France, and I return thanks also to those who have advised me to remain. But I have bethought me that if I remain, I see no danger of my kingdom being lost, for my lady mother, the queen, has no lack of men to defend it. And I have also considered that the barons of this country say that if I go

---

[1] Peasants of the country, of mixed Syrian and European race, were called "poulains;" literally, colts.

away the kingdom of Jerusalem is lost, and that no one
will venture to remain here after I am gone. I have
therefore resolved that at no price would I abandon the
kingdom of Jerusalem, which I came to conquer and
preserve. My decision, therefore, is taken to remain
here for the present. So now, I say to you men of
quality who are here, and to all other knights who may
be willing to stay with me, that you come and speak to
me frankly; and I will give you so much that the fault
will not be mine, but yours, if you do not stay."

Many of those who heard these words were as if stu-
pefied, and many shed tears.

The king, it is said, commanded his brothers to return
to France. I know not if it was at their own request or
by the king's pleasure. It was towards St. John's day
that the king uttered these words to announce his intention of remaining. And it came to pass that on St.
James s day—whose pilgrim I was, and who had worked
me many favours—the king came again from mass to his
own chamber, and summoned those of his council who
had remained with him, to wit, Monseigneur Peter the
chamberlain, who was the most upright and loyal man I
ever saw in the king's household; Monseigneur Geoffrey de Sargines, good knight and prudent; Monseigneur Giles le Brun, good knight and prudent, upon
whom the king had conferred the baton of constable of
France, after the death of Monseigneur Imbert de
Beaujeu, the man of worth. To these the king spoke
after this manner, in a loud tone, as if vexed :—

"Sirs, it is now a month since it was known that I
was going to stay, and I have not yet heard you say that
you have engaged any knights."

"Sire," they replied, "we cannot help it; for every
one makes himself so dear, because they want to go

away to their own country, that we dare not give them what they ask."

"And whom could you find on easier terms?"

"Certes, sire, the seneschal of Champagne; but we dare not give even him what he asks."

I was in the king's chamber, and heard these words. Then the king said: "Call the seneschal here." I went to him, and knelt down, but he made me take a seat, and said to me: "Seneschal, you know how much I have always loved you, but my people tell me that they find you hard. How is this?"

"Sire," I replied, "I cannot help it; for you know that I was taken upon the water, and that there remained to me nothing, but I lost all I had."

Then he asked me how much I wanted, and I said that I wanted 2000 livres until Easter, being two-thirds of the year.

"Tell me, now," said he, "have you made offers to any knights?"

I replied, "Yes, to Monseigneur Peter de Pontmolain and two other bannerets, who cost each 400 livres until Easter."

Then he counted on his fingers, and said: "That is 1200 livres your new knights will cost."

"Consider, sire," I observed, "that I shall need 800 livres to procure horses and arms, and to maintain my knights; for you do not mean us to eat at your table."

Then he said to his people: "Truly, I do not see anything out of the way in that;" and turning to me, he said, "I retain you in my service."

After these things, the king's brothers and the other men of quality who were in Acre got ready their ships. At the moment of leaving Acre, the Count of Poitiers borrowed jewels from those who were going away to

France, and bestowed them lavishly and generously upon us who stayed behind. Both the brothers entreated me to watch over the king, and they told me that of those who were remaining behind there was no one in whom they trusted so much as myself. When the Count of Anjou saw that he must go on board his ship, he exhibited so much sorrow that all were astonished; but for all that he returned to France.

It was no long time after the king's brothers had set out from Acre that messengers from the Emperor Frederick came to the king, and brought him letters of credence, and they told the king that the emperor had sent them to effect our deliverance. They showed the king the letters which the emperor was sending to the sultan (who was dead, though the emperor was not aware of that), and the emperor bade him place entire confidence in his messengers with regard to the king's liberation. Many persons said that it would not have been to our advantage had the messengers found us in prison, for they suspected that the emperor had sent his messengers rather with a view to detain than to free us. The messengers found us already delivered, and so went their way.

While the king was at Acre, the Sultan of Damascus despatched envoys to the king, and complained to him bitterly of the emirs of Egypt, who had put to death his cousin the sultan; and he promised the king that if he would help him he would give over to him the kingdom of Jerusalem which was in his hands. The king decided upon sending an answer to the Sultan of Damascus by the mouth of his own envoys, whom he despatched to the sultan. With these envoys he sent brother Yves, the Breton, of the order of the Dominican friars, who understood Saracen. While they were going from their own lodgings to the sultan's palace, brother Yves saw an old woman crossing the street, who carried in her right hand an open vessel full of fire, and in her left hand a phial full of water. Brother Yves asked her, "What do you mean to do with that?" She replied that with the fire she meant to burn Paradise, and with the water extinguish hell, so that there should be no more of either. And he asked her, "Why do you wish to do that?" "Because I do not wish that any one henceforth shall do what is right for the sake of the rewards of Paradise, or from fear of hell, but simply from love of God, who is so worthy of it, and who can do for us all possible good."

John l'Ermin, the king's armourer, went at that time to Damascus to purchase horn and bird-lime to make cross-bows; and he saw an old man, full of years, seated in the bazaar at Damascus. This old man called to him, and asked if he were a Christian, and he answered, Yes. And the old man said to him: "You Christians must hate each other very much; for once upon a time I saw King Baldwin of Jerusalem, who was a leper, discomfit Saladin, and he had only 300 men-at-arms, while Saladin had 3000. You must therefore be worked upon by your sins to that point that you fall upon us in the fields like so many wild beasts."

Then John l'Ermin told him to hold his tongue about the sins of the Christians, because the sins which the Saracens committed were much greater. And the Saracen retorted that he had answered him like a fool. John asked him in what way. He replied that he would tell him, but that he would first of all put a question to him. And he asked him if he had any children. John answered, "Yes, a son." The Saracen then asked him which would vex him most, a box on the ears from his son, or from another person. John replied that he would be more angry with his son if he struck him than with himself, for instance "Well, then," continued the Saracen, " I make my reply to you in this manner: you Christians are the sons of God, and from His name of Christ are called Christians; and He shows you such great favour that He sends you doctors through whom you know when you are doing right and when you are doing wrong. This is why God is more angry at a small sin committed by you than He is at a great one committed by us, who know nothing and are blind; for we believe that we are quit of our sins if we can wash ourselves in water before we die, for Mohammed has told us that at our death we should be saved by water."

John l'Ermin was in my company once when I went to Paris, after I came back from beyond sea. While we were eating in a tent, a great multitude of poor people begged of us for the love of God, and made a great noise. One of our party commanded and said to one of our valets:—

"Get up, and drive away those beggars."

"Ah!" cried John l'Ermin, "you have said what is not right; for if the king of France were to send us now by his messengers a hundred marks of silver apiece, we should not drive them away; and yet you drive away these envoys, who offer to give you all that any one can give you, that is to say, they ask you to give them something for God, which means that you shall give them of your goods, and they will give you God. And God says with His own mouth that they have power to give Him unto us; and the saints say that the poor can reconcile us unto God, for that, as water extinguishes fire, so do alms extinguish sin. So, let it never happen to you," said John, "to drive away the poor, but rather give unto them, and God will give unto you."

While the king was sojourning at Acre, messengers from the Old Man of the Mountain came to him. When the king returned from mass he sent for them into his presence. The king made them sit down, and in front of the others was an emir, well dressed and handsomely armed; and behind him sat a bachelor, also well appointed, who held in his hand three knives, the blade of one running into the handle of another, because, if the emir had been refused, he would have presented these three knives to the king in token of defiance. Behind him who held the three knives sat another with a shroud twisted round his arm, which likewise he would have presented to the king to bury him in, had he refused the demand of the Old Man of the Mountain.

The king commanded the emir to state his wishes, whereupon the emir handed him his letters of credence, and spoke as follows, " My lord sends me to ask you if you know him." The king replied that he did not know him, for he had never seen him, though he had often heard him spoken of. " Since you have heard my lord spoken of, I am truly astonished that you have not sent him presents, to conciliate his friendship, as the Emperor of Germany, the King of Hungary, the Sultan of Babylon, and the others, do every year, because they know that they can live only so long as it may please my lord. If it is not agreeable to you to do this, release him from the tribute he owes to the Hospital and the Temple, and he will hold himself satisfied." At that time he used to pay tribute to the Temple and the Hospital, because they did not at all fear the assassins, as the Old Man of the Mountain could gain nothing by putting to death the master of

the Temple, or of the Hospital, for he well knew that if
he did kill one of them, another quite as good would
immediately take his place. For that reason he would
not risk his Assassins where there was nothing to be
gained. The king desired the emir to return in the
afternoon.

When the emir returned, he found the king seated in
such wise, that the master of the Temple was on one
side, and the master of the Hospital on the other. Then
the king bade him repeat what he had said to him in
the morning; but the emir replied that he had no intention of repeating it except in the presence of those who
were with the king in the morning. Thereupon the two
masters said to him : " We command you to repeat it."
And he said he would tell them since they commanded
it. The two masters then enjoined him, in the Saracen
tongue, to come and speak to them on the morrow at
the Hospital, and he did so.

Then the two masters told him that his lord was very
bold in daring to send such an insolent message to the
king; and they further told him that, were it not for
the king's sake, to whom they had come as envoys, they
would have had them drowned in the filthy sea of Acre,
in spite of their lord. " And we command you that
you return to your lord, and that you come back here
in a fortnight, and bring to the king, on the part of your
lord, letters and jewels such as may content the king,
and procure you thanks from him."

Within a fortnight the messengers of the Old Man of
the Mountain returned to Acre, and brought to the
king the Old Man's shirt; and they said to the king, on
the part of the Old Man, that it was a token that, as the
shirt is nearer to the body than any other garment, so
the Old Man desired to hold the king nearer to his love

than any other king. And he sent the king his ring,
which was of pure gold, with his name engraved upon
it; and he explained that with this ring he espoused the
king, for he desired that henceforth they should be as
one. Among other curiosities which he sent to the
king was a crystal elephant, very well carved, and an
animal they call a giraffe, also in crystal, different
species of apple in crystal, and backgammon and chess-
boards, and all these were ornamented with amber, and
the amber was attached to the crystal by beautiful fasten-
ings of pure gold. As soon as the envoys opened the
coffers in which these things were packed, it seemed as
if the whole chamber were filled with spices, so fra-
grantly did they smell.

The king sent back these messengers to the Old Man,
and with them a great quantity of jewels, scarlet cloths,
gold cups, and silver horse-bits; and at the same time
he sent brother Yves, the Breton, who understood Saracen. Brother Yves discovered that the Old Man of
the Mountain did not believe in Mohammed, but in the
law of Ali, who was Mohammed's uncle. This Ali
raised Mohammed to the degree of honour he attained,
and when Mohammed had established himself lord of
the people, he despised his uncle, and separated from
him. When Ali saw that, he drew to himself as many
of the people as he could, and taught them another
faith than what they had learnt from Mohammed, whence
it happens that those who believe in the law of Ali
declare that those who believe in the law of Mohammed
are unbelievers; and in like manner those who believe
in the law of Mohammed declare that those who believe
in the law of Ali are unbelievers.

One of the points of the law of Ali is, that, when a
man loses his life in executing the commands of his lord

his soul passes into a happier body than it previously inhabited, wherefore the Assassins do not hesitate to risk their lives when their lord bids them, because they believe that they will be happier after they are dead than they were before.

Another point is, that they believe no man can die before the day that is appointed for him to die; but that is what no man ought to believe, for God has power to prolong or to shorten our lives. It is a point in which the Bedaweens also believe, and for that reason they will not put on armour when they go forth to battle, for they deem that they would be acting contrary to the injunctions of their law. And when they curse their children, they say, "Be thou accursed as the Frank, who puts on armour for fear of death!"

Brother Yves found a book at the head of the Old Man's bed, in which were written several words addressed to St. Peter by our Lord, when he was on earth.

And brother Yves said to him, "Ah! for God's sake, sir, read this book often, for these are truly excellent words."

And he answered that he did so. "For I greatly love Monseigneur St. Peter, for in the beginning of the world the soul of Abel, after he was killed, passed into the body of Noah; and when Noah was dead, it came back into the body of Abraham; and from the body of Abraham, when he was dead, it went into the body of St. Peter, about the time God came upon earth."

When brother Yves heard that, he pointed out to him that his belief was unfounded, and gave him much good instruction, but he would not listen to him. And brother Yves explained all this to the king when he rejoined us. When the Old Man rode out on horseback, there went a crier before him, bearing a Danish battle-axe, with a long handle covered with silver, and stuck all over with knives, and he cried aloud, " Turn aside from before him who carries the death of kings in his hands."

I omitted to tell you the answer the king made to the Sultan of Damascus, and which was in this wise, that he had no intention of going to him until such time as he knew whether or not the emirs of Egypt would make him any amends for the treaty they had broken, and that he would send to them about that matter, and that if they would not renew the treaty they had broken, he would willingly assist him in avenging his cousin, the Sultan of Babylon, who was murdered by the emirs.

While the king was at Acre, he despatched Monseigneur John de Valenciennes into Egypt, who required the emirs to redress the wrongs and outrages they had done to the king. They replied that they would willingly do so, provided the king would ally himself with them against the Sultan of Damascus. Monseigneur John de Valenciennes blamed them greatly for the grievous wrongs they had done to the king, and told them that it would be well, if they wished to soften the king's heart towards them, to send him back all the knights they had detained in prison. And they did so, and in addition they sent him all the bones of the Count of Brienne, to be laid in consecrated ground. When Monseigneur John de Valenciennes returned to Acre with 200 knights, whom he brought back from prison, without reckoning the smaller people, Madame de Sayette, cousin of Count Walter, and sister of Monseigneur Walter Seigneur de Resnel, whose daughter John, Sire de Joinville, took for his wife, after he returned from beyond sea. Madame de Sayette took the bones of

Count Walter, and had them interred with the knights of the Hospital in Acre.   And she had the service performed in such fashion that every knight presented at the offertory a wax-taper, and a silver penny, while the king gave a taper and a bezant, the whole at the charge of Madame de Sayette.   Some persons greatly marvelled at the king doing that, for he had never been known to give any but his own money at the offertory ; but he did so from courtesy.

Among the knights whom Monseigneur John de Valenciennes brought back, I found forty belonging to the Count of Champagne.   I caused coats and surcoats of green cloth to be fashioned for them, and brought them before the king, and besought him to be pleased to do so that they should remain with him.   The king heard what they demanded, but made no reply.   And a knight of his council said that it was not well of me to bring such propositions to the king, for it was at least 7000 livres in excess.   I answered him that he spoke unadvisedly in speaking thus, and that from among us from Champagne we had lost thirty-five knights of the Count of Champagne, all bearing banners, and I said, "The king will not do wisely if he listens to you, in the need he has of knights."   After these words, I began to weep very bitterly ; but. the king bade me be quiet, and he would give them all I asked. The king then received them as I wished, and placed them in my "battle."

The king replied to the messengers from Egypt that he would conclude no treaty with them until they had sent him all the Christian heads which had been suspended round the walls of Babylon, since the time when the Count of Bar and the Count of Montfort were taken prisoners ; and if they did not send him all the children who had been taken and made renegades; and if they did not acquit him of the 200,000 livres which he still owed them. With the envoys of the emirs of Egypt, the king despatched Monseigneur John de Valenciennes, a man of wisdom and valour.

At the commencement of Lent (A.D. 1251), the king prepared to march with all the troops he had to fortify Cæsarea, which the Saracens had destroyed, and which was twelve leagues further on towards Jerusalem. Monseigneur Raoul de Soissons, who had stayed behind sick at Acre, went with the king to fortify Cæsarea. I know not how it happened, except through God's will, that they never did us any damage all that year. While the king was fortifying Cæsarea the messengers to the Tartars came back to us, and we will now tell you of the tidings they brought back with them.

As I said before, while the king was sojourning in Cyprus, messengers from the Tartars came to him, and gave him to understand that they would help him in wresting the kingdom of Jerusalem from the Saracens. The king in his turn despatched messengers to them, by whom he sent them a chapel he had had made in scarlet cloth, and to attract them to our faith he had had embroidered in this chapel the chief articles of our faith, the Annunciation by the Angel, the Nativity, the Baptism with which God was baptized, the whole of the Passion, the Ascension, and the descent of the Holy Ghost. He sent them also chalices, books, and all that was necessary to chant the mass, and two Dominican friars to perform the service before them. The king's envoys landed at the port of Antioch; and from Antioch to the great Khan of the Tartars they found it was a good year of marching, riding ten leagues a day. They discovered that the whole country was subject to the Tartars, and

came across several towns they had destroyed, and great
heaps of human bones. They inquired how the Tartars
had obtained such great power as to have been able to
slay and destroy such a multitude of people, and it was
done in this manner, as they reported to the king. The
Tartars originally came from a huge sandy plain, where
nothing would grow. This plain began at very lofty
and very wonderful rocks at the world's end towards
the east, which rocks have never been crossed by man,
as the Tartars affirm, and they said that within them
are imprisoned the hosts of Gog and Magog, who are to
come forth at the end of the world, when Antichrist shall
come to destroy it. In this plain dwelt the people of
the Tartars, and were subject to Prester John and the
Emperor of Persia, whose lands adjoined their own, and
to several other unbelieving kings, to whom they paid
tribute and service every year, for the sake of pasturing
their cattle, for these were their only means of sub-
sistence. This Prester John, the Emperor of Persia,
and the other kings, held the Tartars in such contempt,
that when they brought their rents, they would not
receive them into their presence, but turned their backs
upon them. Among them was a wise man, who travelled
over all the plains, and spoke to the men in different
places, and pointed out the serfage in which they were
held, and entreated them all to consider how they should
escape from the serfdom in which Prester John held
them. He worked so that he brought them all together
at the end of the plain, over against the country of
Prester John, and showed them all this, and they
answered that he should direct them, and they would
execute his orders. And he told them that they would
never succeed until they had a king and lord over them;
and he taught them in what manner they should choose

a king, and they agreed to it. And the manner was in
this wise, of the fifty-two tribes that there were, each
one was to bring him an arrow, which they had marked
with their own name; and with the consent of all the
people it was resolved that these fifty-two arrows should
be placed before a child only five years old, and that
whichever one the child should first take hold of should
fix the tribe whence the king was to be chosen. As
soon as the child had taken up one of the arrows, the
wise man made the other tribes fall back, and it was
decided that the men of the tribe from whom the king
was to be taken should pick out fifty-two of the wisest
and best men. When they were selected, each brought
an arrow marked with his name. Then it was agreed
that he whose arrow the child should lay hold of should
be made king. And the child took the one that belonged to the Wise Man who had counselled them, and
the people were so delighted that every one displayed
great joy. He bade them be silent. "Sirs, if you wish
that I should be your king, you must swear to me by
Him who created the heaven and the earth, that you
will keep my commandments." And they sware unto
him.

The institutions he bestowed upon them were with
the intent of keeping the people in peace, such as that
no one should seize his neighbour's property; that no
one should strike another if he would not lose his hand;
and that no one should have connection with his neighbour's wife or daughter, if he would not lose his life or
his hand. And many other good laws he imposed upon
them in order to have peace.

After he had introduced order and organization among
them, he said to them, "Sirs, the worst enemy we have
is Prester John, and I command you that to-morrow

you be prepared to attack him. If it come to pass, which God forbid, that he discomfits us, let every one do the best he can for himself; but if we discomfit him, I command that the fighting shall last for three days and three nights, and that no one shall be so bold as to put his hand to the booty, but only to slay the men, for after we have gained the victory, I will divide the booty among you so fairly and loyally, that every one shall be satisfied." To this they all agreed.

On the morrow they attacked their enemies, and, as it pleased God, completely routed them. All whom they found with arms in their hands, and able to defend themselves, they slew outright; but those whom they found in the garb of ministers of religion, such as priests and other servants of religion, they did not slay. The rest of the people in the land of Prester John, who were not at that battle, placed themselves in entire subjection to them.

A prince of one of the tribes before mentioned disappeared for fully three months without any news being heard of him; and when he came back he had neither hunger nor thirst, for he believed that he had been absent for not more than one night. The tidings he brought back were that he had come upon a very elevated tract of ground, and therein he had seen the most beautiful people he had ever beheld, the best clad and the most handsomely decked out; and at the further end of this lofty ground he had seen a king still fairer to look upon than the others, better dressed, more handsomely decked out, and seated upon a golden throne. At his right hand sat six crowned kings, splendidly decorated with precious stones, and as many on his left hand. Near him, on his right hand, was a queen on her knees, who spoke to him and besought him to think of his people. On his left there was a very fine looking man, who had two wings as resplendent as the sun; and round about the king were a great number of beautiful beings with wings.

The king called this prince, and said to him: "Thou art come from the army of the Tartars?"

And he replied: "Sire, in truth I have just come from it."

"Thou wilt go back to that army, and thou shalt say to it, that thou hast seen me, who am the Lord of heaven and earth; and thou shalt say to it, that it must render thanks unto me for the victory which I have conferred upon it over Prester John and his people. And thou shalt moreover say unto it, from me, that I give it power to bring the whole earth under subjection."

"Sire," replied the prince, "how will it believe me?"

"Thou shalt say to it, that it must believe thee by this token, that thou shalt go and do battle with the Emperor of Persia with no more than three hundred of thy people; and in order that your great king may believe that I have power to do all things, I will give thee strength to overthrow the Emperor of Persia, who shall oppose thee with more than three hundred thousand armed men. Before thou goest forth to give him battle, thou shalt require of thy king that he bestow upon thee the priests and ministers of religion whom he took captive in the battle; and what they teach thee thou shalt believe steadfastly, thou and all thy people."

"Sire," replied he, "I know not which way to go back, unless thou guidest me."

And the king turned to a mighty array of knights so well armed that it was a marvel to behold them, and called and said: "George, come hither!"

And he came and knelt down. And the king said: "Arise; conduct me this man to the camp in safety."

And he did so in one instant. As soon as his people heard this, they and the whole camp also manifested so great a joy that it cannot be told. He asked the great king for the priests, who gave them to him; and this prince and all his people received their teachings in such good part, that they were all baptized. After this he took three hundred armed men and made them confess and prepare themselves, and marched to give battle to the Emperor of Persia, whom he discomfited and expelled from his kingdom. The emperor fled away to the kingdom of Jerusalem, and he it was who routed our people and made prisoner Count Walter of Brienne, as you will hear by-and-bye.

The people of this Christian prince were so great, that the king's messengers told us they had in their camp eight hundred chapels on wheels. Their manner of living is such that they eat no bread, but subsist on flesh and milk. The best flesh they have is that of the horse; and they lay it in slices in brine, and afterwards dry it until they can cut it like black bread. The best drink they have and the strongest is mare's milk flavoured with herbs. A present had been made to the great Khan of the Tartars of a horse loaded with flour, which had come from a distance of three months' march, and he gave it to the king's messengers.

There are a great many Christians among them who believe in the religion of the Greeks, both those of whom we have spoken and others. These they send against Saracens when they want to make war upon Saracens; and they send Saracens against Christians when they want to make war upon Christians. Every description of women, without children, accompany them to war.

and they give pay to the women as well as to the men, according to their vigour.   And the king's messengers recounted that the men and women who receive pay ate together in the houses of the men of quality, to whom they belonged;   and the men dared not, in any way, touch the women, because of the law their first king had given them.   They carry to their camp all kinds of flesh, for they eat of every kind.   The women who have children take care of them, look after them, and prepare food for those who go to the battle.   They put raw flesh between their saddles and the flaps of their garments, and when the blood has been thoroughly pressed out they eat it raw.   What they cannot eat they throw into a leathern bag;   and when they are hungry they open the bag, and always eat the stalest first.   I saw a Kharismian who had been in the Emperor of Persia's army, and who guarded us in prison;   when he opened his bag we used to hold our noses, because we could not bear the stench that issued from the bag.

Let us now return to our subject, and tell how when the great Khan of the Tartars had received the messengers and presents, he invited, under promise of safe conduct, several kings who had not yet submitted themselves to his mercy;   and he had the chapel pitched for them, and spoke to them after this fashion,—" Sirs, the King of France has come under subjection to us, and this is the tribute he sends us;   and if you do not submit yourselves to our mercy we will send for him to come and vanquish you."   A considerable number of those who were present, from fear of the King of France, made their submission to this King of the Tartars.

His messengers accompanied those of the king, and brought to the King of France letters from their great king, couched in this wise,—" Peace is a good thing;

for in a land of peace those who go upon four legs crop the herb undisturbed; and those who go upon two till the earth, whose fruits come peacefully. And we tell thee this to warn thee; for thou canst not have peace if thou have it not with us; and such and such kings (naming several) we have put to the edge of the sword. Therefore, we enjoin thee, that every year thou sendest us a goodly store of thy silver and of thy gold, and so shalt thou retain us as thy friend; and if thou dost not do this we will destroy thee and thy people, as we did unto those we have above named." Be sure the sainted king sorely repented that he had sent any envoy thither.

CHAPTER XI.

WHILE the king was fortifying Cæsarea there arrived in camp Monseigneur Alenars de Senaingan, who told us that he had built his ship in the kingdom of Norway, which is at the end of the world, towards the west; and that in the voyage he made to the king he had sailed round Spain and passed through the Straits of Morocco. He had encountered grievous perils before he reached us; the king retained him and nine other knights with him. He related to us that in the land of Norway the nights are so short in summer that there is no night in which you cannot see, at the same time, the light of the day that is over and that of the day which is beginning. He and his people betook themselves to hunting lions, and they caught several, with very great danger. For they went and hurled javelins at the lions, galloping as fast as they could; and when they fired the lion would spring towards them, and in an instant he would have overtaken and devoured them had they not let drop a piece of old cloth; when the lion stopped, tore the cloth to pieces, and swallowed it, for he fancied he had got a man. While he was rending this cloth another would fire at him, and the lion would leave the cloth and pursue

the hunter, and as soon as he let fall a piece of cloth the
lion threw himself upon that. By this means they killed
the lion, by piercing him with darts.

While the king was fortifying Cæsarea, Monseigneur
Philip de Toucy came to him, and the king claimed him
as a cousin, because he was sprung from one of the
sisters of King Philip (Philip Augustus), whom the
emperor (Andronicus of Constantinople) himself took to
wife. The king retained him, with nine other knights,
for the space of one year, when he departed and returned
to Constantinople, whence he had come. He related to
the king that the Emperor of Constantinople and the
other men of quality who were in Constantinople, were
at that time allied to a people called Comans, in order
to obtain their aid against Vataces, the Emperor of the
Greeks. As a guarantee that each would assist the
other in good faith, the emperor and the other men of
quality who were with him were obliged to let themselves be bled, and to put their blood in a large silver
bowl. And the King of the Comans, and the other men
of quality who were with him, did the same on their
part, and, mixing their blood with that of our people,
poured upon it wine and water, and drank of it, as did
our people likewise; then they said they were brothers
by blood. Moreover, they made a dog pass between our
people and themselves, and they cut the dog to pieces
with their swords, as also did our people; and they said
that they ought to be cut to pieces in like manner if
they failed one another.

He related to us yet another great marvel. While
he was in their camp a knight of much means died, and
they dug for him a broad and deep trench in the earth,
and they seated him, very nobly attired, on a chair, and
placed by his side the best horse and the best sergeant

he had, both alive. The sergeant, before he was placed in the grave with his lord, went round to the King of the Comans, and the other men of quality, and while he was taking leave of them they threw into his scarf a large quantity of silver and gold, and said to him, " When I come to the other world thou shalt return to me what I now entrust to thee." And he replied, " I will gladly do so."

The great King of the Comans confided to him a letter addressed to their first king, in which he informed him that this worthy man had led a good life and had served him faithfully, and begged him to reward him for his services. When this was done, they placed him in the grave with his lord and the horse, both alive; then they threw over the trench boards closely fitted together, and the whole army ran to pick up stones and earth, so that before they slept they had erected a great mound over it, in remembrance of those who were interred.

While the king was fortifying Cæsarea, I went into his tent to see him. As soon as he saw me enter his tent, where he was conversing with the legate, he rose and drew me aside, and said, " You are aware that I retained you only till Easter; I pray you, therefore, tell me what I shall give you from Easter, for one year."

And I replied, that I did not wish him to give me any more of his money than he had already given, but that I wished to make another compact with him, " because," said I, " you always get angry if any one asks you for anything. I wish you to promise me that if I ask anything of you in the course of the year, you will not get angry; and if you refuse me I will not be angry on my part."

When he heard that he laughed aloud, and said he

retained me on that condition. He then led me to the legate and his council and repeated to them the compact we had made; and they were very merry over it, because I was the man of the highest quality in the camp.

I will now tell you how I ordered and arranged my affairs during the four years I remained after the king's brothers had gone away. I had two chaplains with me who recited my Hours to me; one of them chanted my mass as soon as the dawn of day appeared, while the other waited until my own knights and those of my "battle" were up. When I had heard my mass, I went about with the king. When the king was disposed to take a ride, I accompanied him. Sometimes it happened that messengers came to him, in consequence of which we had to work all the morning.

My bed was placed in my tent so that no one could enter without seeing me lying in it; and this I had done to remove all wrongful suspicion of commerce with women. When St. Remy's day (October 1st) was nigh at hand I purchased pigs to fill my styes, and sheep to fill my folds, and flour and wine to supply the household during the whole winter; and I did so because all kinds of merchandise become dearer in winter, because of the sea, which is then more stormy than in summer. And I purchased a hundred casks of wine, and caused always the best to be drunk first; and I had the wine of the valets well watered—but less water was put in the wine for the squires. At my own table, in front of each knight, was placed a large bottle of wine and a large bottle of water; and they diluted it as they pleased.

The king had assigned to my "battle" fifty knights; at every repast I had ten of these knights at my table with my own ten; and they eat facing one another, according to the custom of the country, and sat down on

L

the ground upon mats. Every time the alarm was given
I sent out fifty-four knights, who were called *dizeniers*
because each of them commanded ten men, each time
we rode forth to battle ; on our return the fifty knights
dined at my house. At all the annual festivals I invited
all the men of quality in the camp ; wherefore the king
was sometimes obliged to borrow some of those whom I
had invited.

You shall hear now of some of the judgments and
sentences which I heard pronounced at Cæsarea while
the king tarried there.

In the first place we will tell you of a knight who was
caught in a house of ill fame, and who was allowed to
choose one of two things, according to the custom of the
country. The alternative was this : either that the
wanton should lead him through the camp in his shirt,
shamefully bound by a rope, or that he should forfeit
his horse and his arms, and be expelled from the camp.
The knight left his horse and arms with the king, and
went his way. I begged the king to give me the horse
for a poor gentleman who was in the camp. And the
king replied, that my request was not reasonable, for
the horse was well worth eighty *livres*. " Why have
you broken our compact by losing your temper about
what I asked of you ? "

The king answered laughing, " Ask for what you
please, I will not lose my temper."

For all that, I did not get the horse for the poor
gentleman.

The second judgment was in this wise. The knights
of our " battle " were hunting a wild animal called a
gazelle, which is something like a roebuck. The brethren of the Hospital rushed at our knights, hustled
them, and drove them off. I complained to the master

of the Hospital, who replied that he would do me justice according to the usage of the Holy Land, which was that he would make the brethren who had committed the outrage take their meals upon the ground, seated on their cloaks, until such time as those to whom the outrage had been offered should forgive them. The master kept his promise; and when we saw that they had eaten for some time upon their cloaks, I went to the master and found him at table, and I prayed him to allow the brethren to rise who were eating on their cloaks before him; and the knights to whom the wrong had been done also besought him. But he answered that he would do nothing of the kind, for he would not have the brethren offer insults to those who came on pilgrimage to the Holy Land. When I heard that I seated myself beside the brethren, and began to eat with them; and I told him I would not rise until the brethren also rose. He replied that I was putting violence upon him, and granted my request; and he made me and the knights who were with me, sit at meat with himself; and the brethren went to dine at table with their comrades.

A third judgment which I saw rendered at Caesarea was in this way. One of the king's sergeants having laid his hand upon a knight belonging to my corps, I went and complained to the king, who said that it seemed to him I might very well desist from my complaint, for the sergeant had only pushed the knight. I told him that I would not desist, and that if he did not do me justice I would leave his service, since his sergeants lifted their hands against knights. He then consented to do me justice after the usages of the country, which were such that the sergeant came to my tent barefooted, in his drawers, and without any other article of dress, and with a naked sword in his hand, and knelt down before the knight, and said to him, " Sir, I make reparation to you for having laid my hand upon you, and I have brought you this sword that you may cut off my hand, if so it please you." And I prayed the knight to pardon him, and he did so.

The fourth punishment was in this manner. Brother Hugh de Jouy, marshal of the Temple, was despatched to the Sultan of Damascus by the master of the Temple, to effect an agreement respecting some land which the Temple held, but of which the sultan wished to have one-half, and that the Temple should 'have the other half. The agreement was concluded on the condition that the king consented' to it. And brother Hugh brought with him an emir from the sultan, and the agreement made out in writing to be authentic. The master told this to the king, at which he was greatly moved, and said that it was very presumptuous on his part to have concluded or negotiated any sort of agreement with the sultan without first speaking to him ; and the king insisted that reparation should be made to him. The reparation was that the king caused the hangings of three of his tents to be raised, and all the common people of the army came who wished to witness the scene ; and thither came the master of the Temple and his knights, barefooted, right through the camp, because their tents were outside the camp. The king made the master of the Temple and the sultan's messenger sit down before him, and the king said to the master, in a loud tone of voice, " Master, you will tell the sultan's messenger that you are grieved at having made a treaty with him without speaking to me about it ; and, because you did not first mention it to me, you hold him discharged from all that he promised you, and you return him his promises."

The master took the agreement and handed it to the emir. Then the king told the master to stand up, and make all his brethren do the same; and he did so.

"Now kneel down, and make me a reparation for having acted contrary to my pleasure."

The master knelt down and held out the skirt of his cloak to the king, and placed at the king's disposal all they possessed to select his own reparation, according as he himself wished to regulate it.

"I declare, first of all," said the king, "that brother Hugh, who negotiated this agreement, is banished from the entire kingdom of Jerusalem."

Neither the master, nor a brother Hugh, who was the king's gossip, as father-in-law of the Count of Alençon, born at Châtel-Pelerin, nor the queen, nor others, could render any aid to brother Hugh de Jony, and avert from him the necessity of withdrawing from the Holy Land and the kingdom of Jerusalem.

While the king was fortifying Cæsarea, the Egyptian envoys returned to him and brought him the treaty, drawn up as the king had desired; and the convention between the king and them was to the effect, that on a day which was named the king was to go to Jaffa, and that on the same day the emirs of Egypt were bound by oath to be at Gaza, to give over the kingdom of Jerusalem. The king and the principal men of the army confirmed by oath the treaty which the envoys had brought to us, and we pledged ourselves by oath to help them against the Sultan of Damascus.

When the Sultan of Damascus learnt that we had allied ourselves with the rulers of Egypt, he sent 4000 Turks, well appointed, to Gaza, whither they of Egypt were to come, because he knew that if they could make a junction with us he was likely to suffer. The king, however, did not the less set out to proceed to Jaffa. When the Count of Jaffa heard that the king was coming, he put his castle into such a condition that any one could see that it was a place quite tenable; for on each of the battlements, of which there were 500, there was suspended his shield, with his arms and a flag, which was a pleasant sight to behold; for his arms were *or*, with a cross *pâtée gules*. We pitched our tents round the castle in the fields, and we surrounded the castle, which is situated on the sea, from one shore to the other. Straightway the king applied himself to fortifying a new town round the whole castle, from one shore to the other; and many a time I saw the king himself carrying the hod in the trenches, to gain the indulgence.

The emirs of Egypt failed to fulfil the convention they had made with us, for they dared not come to Gaza because of the troops of the Sultan of Damascus which were there. However, they kept word with us so far that they sent the king all the Christian heads which they had suspended from the walls of the castle of Cairo since the time when the Count of Bar and the Count of Montfort were taken: the king had them laid in consecrated ground. They sent him also the children that had been taken at the same time with the king, which they did with regret, as these children had already renounced their faith. And with these things they presented the king with an elephant, which he sent to France.

While we were tarrying at Jaffa, an emir, who belonged to the party of the Sultan of Damascus, came to cut down the corn near a village about three leagues from the camp. It was resolved that we should attack him, but when he saw us coming he took to flight. As he fled a young valet of gentle blood singled him out for pursuit, and hurled two of his knights to the earth without breaking his lance, and finally struck the emir so that he broke off the iron part in his body.

These messengers from the emirs of Egypt prayed the king to fix a day for receiving them, and they would come without fault. The king determined not to refuse them, and appointed a day; and they promised him on their oath that on that day the emirs should be at Gaza.

While we were looking forward to the day which the king had appointed the emirs of Egypt, the Count of Eu, who had not yet been knighted, came to the camp, and brought with him Monseigneur Arnold de Guines, the good knight, and his two brothers, with nine other knights. He remained in the king's service, who made him a knight.

At that time there came to the camp the Prince of Antioch and the princess his mother. The king showed him much respect, and knighted him with great honours. His age was not more than sixteen, but never have I met with a child so sensible. He asked the king to hear him speak in the presence of his mother, and the king granted his request. The words he addressed to the king in his mother's presence were to this effect :—

"Sire, it is very true that my mother is entitled to hold me yet four years under her tutelage; but it is not right that she should therefore allow my land to be lost or fall to decay; and I say this, sire, because the city of Antioch is going to ruin in her hands. Therefore I entreat you, sire, to pray her to supply me with money with which I may go to the succour of my friends who are there, and aid them. And, sire, she may do it with advantage, for if I remain with her in the town of Tripoli, it will not be without great expenditure, and this expenditure will be incurred for nothing."

The king listened to him with pleasure, and used all

his influence with his mother to give him as much
as he could extract from her. As soon as he had
quitted the king, he went off to Antioch, where he
was well received. With the king's consent, he quar-
tered his arms, which are *gules*, with the arms of France,
because the king had made him a knight.

With the prince came three minstrels from Upper
Armenia. They were brothers, and were going to
Jerusalem on a pilgrimage, and they had three horns,
the ends of which came round towards their faces.
When they began to blow their horns, you would have
said that it was the song of the swan from the pond;
and they gave forth the sweetest and most touching
melodies, so that it was a marvel to hear them. They
all three made wonderful jumps; for a cloth was spread
beneath their feet, and they threw a complete somerset, so that their feet came down straight upon the
cloth. Two of them threw the somerset backwards,
and the eldest likewise; but when he had to throw it
forward he crossed himself, for he feared that he would
break his neck in turning over.

CHAPTER XII.

T is a pleasant thing to tell of the bearing of the Count of Brienne, who was Count of Jaffa for many years, and by his vigour long defended it ; and in a great measure he lived by what he won from the Saracens and the enemies of the faith. Whence it chanced that once upon a time he routed a large party of Saracens who were conveying a great quantity of cloth of gold and silk, the whole of which he carried off; and when he had secured it, he divided the whole of it at Jaffa among his knights without keeping anything to himself. It was his custom when he had quitted his knights to shut himself up in his chapel, where he remained a long time in prayer before he went to lie down beside his wife, who was a very excellent and sensible lady, and sister to the King of Cyprus.

The Emperor of Persia, named Barbaquan, whom one of the Tartar princes had overthrown, as I have already described, came with his army into the kingdom of Jerusalem, and took the fort of Tabarie, which had been built by Monseigneur Eudes de Montbéliard, the constable, who was lord of Tabarie through his wife. He wrought great evil upon our people, for he ravaged all the country round Châtel-Pelerin, and round Acre, and round Sefed, and even round Jaffa; and when he had committed all these ravages he directed his march to Gaza to join the Sultan of Babylon, who was expected there, to injure and molest our people. The barons of the country and the patriarch resolved that they would go and give him battle before the Sultan of Babylon could come up; and to help them they sent for the Sultan of Emessa, one of the best knights in all the lands of the paynim, and to whom they showed so much honour in Acre that they laid down cloths of gold and silk for him to walk upon. They went as far as Jaffa, our people and the sultan with them. The patriarch held under excommunication Count Walter, because he refused to give him up a tower he had in Jaffa, and which was called the Patriarch's Tower. Our people entreated Count Walter to go with them to give battle to the Emperor of Persia; and he said he would do so readily if the patriarch would give him absolution until their return. The patriarch refused to do anything of the kind; but, nevertheless, Count Walter went forth and marched along with them. Our people formed three divisions, of which Count Walter had one, the Sultan of Emessa another, and the patriarch, with those of the country, the third. In the Count of Brienne's corps were the Knights Hospitallers. They rode along until they saw the enemy right before them. As soon as our people saw them they halted, and the enemy also formed themselves into three battles. While the Kharasmians were drawing up their corps, Count Walter came to our people and cried: " Sirs, for God's sake, let us attack them, for we are giving them time while we are halting here." But no one would listen to him. When Count Walter saw that, he came to the patriarch and begged him to give him absolution, as before mentioned; but the patriarch would do nothing of the kind. With the Count of Brienne there was a valiant clerk, who had been Bishop of Ramleh, and had performed many gallant deeds of prowess in the count's company; and he said to the count :—

"Let not your conscience be troubled because the patriarch will not absolve you, for he is wrong and you are right, and I absolve you in the name of the Father, the Son, and the Holy Ghost. Let us now have at them !"

Then they drove their spurs in, and attacked the division of the Emperor of Persia, which was in the front, and there was a great multitude of people slain on either side, and Count Walter was taken, for all our people fled so disgracefully that many in their terror were drowned in the sea. This panic seized them because one of the Emperor of Persia's corps attacked the Sultan of Emessa, who defended himself against them with such spirit that, of 2000 Turks he took with him into action, there remained to him only 280 when he quitted the field of battle.

The emperor resolved that he would go and besiege the sultan in his castle of Emessa, because it seemed to him that he could not hold out long after losing so many of his people. When the sultan saw that, he went to his people, and said he should go forth and give battle to the enemy; for if he suffered himself to be besieged he should be lost. He so arranged it, that he sent all his people who were badly armed, by a valley that was out of sight, and as soon as they heard the sultan's drums beat they threw themselves upon the emperor's camp, from the rear, and began to slay the women and children. As soon as the emperor, who had marched into the plain to combat the sultan, whom he saw before him, heard the cries of his people, he returned to his camp to succour the women and children; whereupon the sultan rushed upon him and his army, so that it ensued that of the 25,000 they were at the commencement there remained neither man nor woman.

Before the Emperor of Persia proceeded against Emessa he brought Count Walter before Jaffa; and they hanged him by the arms to a forked pole, and said they would not take him down until they had the castle of Jaffa. While he was hanging by the arms he called out to those of the castle, that no matter what torture was inflicted upon himself not to give up the town; and that if they did give it up he would himself put every one of them to death.

When the emperor saw that, he sent Count Walter to Babylon, and made a present of him to the sultan, as well as of the master of the hospital, and of several other prisoners he had taken. Those who conducted the count to Babylon were three hundred strong, and these were not slain when the emperor perished before Emessa. And these Kharasmians fought against us on the Friday, when they attacked us on foot. Their banners were red, and were attached near the head of the lance, and on their lances they made, of hair, what looked like the heads of devils.

Many of the merchants of Babylon besought the sultan to do them justice on Count Walter for the great mischief he had wrought them; and the sultan gave them permission to avenge themselves. And they went and slew him in the prison, and made a martyr of him; wherefore we are bound to believe that he is in heaven among the other martyrs.

The Sultan of Damascus took his people, who were at Gaza, and marched into Egypt. The emirs came to give him battle. The sultan's division discomfited the

emirs' corps with which he was engaged, but the other
corps of the emirs of Egypt defeated the rear-guard of
the Sultan of Damascus. So the sultan returned to
Gaza, wounded on the head and hand. But before he
left Gaza the emirs of Egypt sent messengers to him,
and made peace with him; and they failed us in all our
conventions, and from that time forth we were never at
peace or truce with either those of Damascus or those
of Babylon. And you must know that when we were
at our greatest possible strength under arms, we were
never more than 1400.

While the king was encamped before Jaffa, the Master of St. Lazarus discovered, near Ramleh, distant
three long leagues, cattle and other property, of which
he thought to make booty; and, as he held no rank in
the army, but did as he pleased, he went off without first
speaking to the king. When he had collected his spoils,
the Saracens attacked and so completely discomfited
him, that of all the people he had with him, in his own
corps, there escaped only four. As soon as he entered
the camp he began crying out, "To arms!" I went
and armed myself, and begged the king to allow me to
go forth; he gave me permission, and commanded me to
take with me the Templars and the Hospitallers. When
we reached the spot, we found that some other Saracens,
who were strangers, had gone down into the valley
where the Master of St. Lazarus had been defeated.
While these Saracen strangers were examining the dead
the master of the king's crossbow-men attacked them,
and before we could get up with them our people had
routed them and slain several.

One of the king's sergeants and one of the Saracens
threw each other to the ground with a lance-thrust.
Another of the king's sergeants, who saw that, took the

two horses and led them away to steal them; and, that he might not be seen, he concealed himself among the walls of the town of Ramleh. While he was leading them along, an old reservoir over which he passed gave way under him, and himself and his three horses fell to the bottom, and word was brought to me. I went to see for myself, and observed that the sides of the reservoir were crumbling in upon them, and in a little more they would have been entirely buried. So we returned without losing any, save those who had been lost by the Master of St. Lazarus.

As soon as the Sultan of Damascus had made peace with the emirs of Egypt he sent orders to his people, who were at Gaza, to return to him, and they did so. They passed in front of our camp, within two leagues' distance, but never did they venture to attack us, though there were 20,000 Saracens and 10,000 Beda-weens. Before they came opposite to our camp the master of the king's cross-bowmen and his corps observed them for three days and nights, lest they should throw themselves unexpectedly upon our camp.

On St. John's Day (May 6th, 1253), which was after Easter, the king heard his sermon. While it was being preached, a sergeant of the master of the cross-bowmen entered the chapel, armed at all points, and told him that the Saracens had surrounded the master. I asked the king to let me go, and he granted me permission, but desired me to take four or five hundred men-at-arms, and named those whom he wished me to take.

As soon as we issued from the camp, the Saracens, who had got round between the master of the crossbow-men and the camp, drew off towards an emir who was posted on some rising ground facing the master, with at least a thousand men-at-arms. Then began a combat

between the Saracens and the sergeants of the master
of the crossbow-men, 280 strong; for whenever the
emir saw that these people were hard pressed, he sent
them succour to such an extent that they forced our
sergeants back upon the main body; and when the
master saw that his people were being roughly handled
he sent them 100 or 120 men-at-arms, who drove the
enemy back upon the main body of the emir's troops.

While we were there, the legate and the barons of the
country, who had remained with the king, told him that
it was very foolish to place me in peril; and by their
advice the king ordered myself, and the master of the
cross-bowmen also, to return to camp. The Turks pursued their march, and we retraced our steps to the
camp.

Many persons marvelled that the Saracens did not
come forward to attack us, and some said they only
abstained from doing so because both themselves and
their horses had been half-starved at Gaza, where they
had passed nearly a whole year.

After these Saracens had withdrawn from before
Jaffa they appeared before Acre, and threatened the
Seigneur d'Assur, who was constable of the kingdom
of Jerusalem, that they would destroy the gardens of
the town if he did not send them 50,000 bezants; and
he answered that he would send them not one. Then
they placed their troops in array, and marched along
the sands of Acre till they came so near to the town as
to be within range of a shot from a fixed cross-bow.
The Sire d'Assur issued forth from the town and took
post on Mount St. John, by the cemetery of St. Nicholas,
in order to defend the gardens. Our foot-sergeants
also marched out and began to harass the enemy with
bows and cross-bows.

The Sire d'Assur called to him a knight, named Monseigneur John le Grand, and commanded him to withdraw the light troops that had issued from the town, lest they should run into danger.

While he was bringing them back a Saracen began to call out to him in Saracen that he would joust with him if he liked; and he replied that he would do so willingly. As Monseigneur John was going towards the Saracen to joust with him he looked towards his left hand and observed a small body of Turks, about eight in number, who had halted to witness the joust. Turning from the Saracen, he went at the party of Turks, who were quietly waiting to see the jousting, and running his spear through one of them laid him dead at his feet. When the others saw that they fell upon him as he was making his way back to our people, and one of them struck him a heavy blow with a mace upon his steel cap, but, as he passed, Monseigneur John gave him a sword-cut upon the turban with which his head was enfolded, and made it fly into the middle of the field. They wear these turbans when in battle because they stand a powerful sword-cut. One of the other Turks spurred towards him, meaning to catch him between the shoulders with his spear, but Monseigneur John saw the lance coming and avoided the thrust. At the moment the Saracen was passing Monseigneur John gave him a back-hander with his sword across the arm, that made his lance fly out of his hand. In this manner he fell back, bringing with him his foot-soldiers; and these three feats he performed before the Seigneur d'Assur and the men of quality who were in Acre, and in the eyes of all the women who were upon the walls to see what was doing.

When this multitude of Saracens who had passed

before Jaffa, without daring to engage with us, or with the garrison of Acre, heard, what was true enough, that the king was causing the town of Sayette to be fortified by a handful of troops, they turned their march in that direction. When Monseigneur Simon de Montbéliard, who was master of the king's cross-bowmen, and commander of the king's troops at Sayette, received notice of the approach of that host, he retired into the castle of Sayette, which is very strong, and surrounded on all sides by the sea, and he did so because he saw clearly that he could not oppose the enemy. He placed in security with himself as many persons as he could, but they were very few, for the castle was exceedingly small. The Saracens rushed into the town, meeting with no resistance, for it was not entirely inclosed. They slaughtered upwards of 2000 of our people, and with all the booty they gathered there they went off to Damascus.

When the king heard these tidings, he was much incensed, and sought how he could retrieve the mischance; and the barons of the country easily found a means, because the king had been desirous of fortifying an eminence on which there formerly stood a fortress in the time of the Machabees. This castle is on the road from Jaffa to Jerusalem. The barons of those parts were opposed to rebuilding the walls of the castle, because it was five leagues from the sea, for which reason supplies could not have reached us from the sea without risk of being intercepted by the Saracens, who were stronger than we were. When the news from Sayette arrived at the camp, reporting the destruction of the town, the barons of the country came to the king and said to him that it would be more to his honour to refortify the town of Sayette, which the Saracens had destroyed, than to erect a new fortress, and the king assented.

M

While the king was at Jaffa, he was informed that the Sultan of Damascus would readily permit him to go to Jerusalem with a trustworthy safe-conduct. The king held a grand council upon the subject, and the result was that not one advised the king to go up, because he must have left the city in the hands of the Saracens.

A case in illustration was pointed out to the king. When the great King Philip (Philip Augustus) quitted Acre to return to France, he left all his troops behind in camp, under the command of Duke Hugh of Burgundy, grandfather of the duke who died last. While the duke tarried at Acre, and King Richard also, news were brought to them that they could take Jerusalem next day if they chose, because all the chivalry of the Sultan of Damascus had gone to aid him in a war he was waging against another sultan. They drew up their forces, the King of England forming the first division, and the Duke of Burgundy the second, with the people of the King of France. While the King of England was in the hope that he was about to take the city, word came to him from the duke's camp not to advance any further, for the duke was marching in retreat, for no other motive than to prevent it being said that the English had taken Jerusalem. While he was engaged in this conference, one of his knights cried out to him: "Sire, sire, come here, and I will show you Jerusalem." But when he heard that, he held his shield up before his eyes, and, with tears, prayed to our Lord: "Fair sire God, I beseech Thee not to suffer me to behold Thy Holy City, seeing that I cannot deliver it out of the hands of Thine enemies."

This example was pointed out to the king, because if he, who was the greatest king in Christendom, accomplished his pilgrimage without rescuing the city from God's enemies, all other kings and pilgrims who might come after him, would content themselves with executing the pilgrimage in the same manner as the King of France had done, and would not trouble themselves about the recovery of Jerusalem.

King Richard performed so many exploits when he was beyond sea, that when the horses of the Saracens shied at a bush, their masters said to them, "Do you fancy," cried they to their horses, "that it is King Richard of England?" And when their children were troublesome, they would say to them, "Peace, peace, or I will fetch King Richard, who will kill you."

The Duke of Burgundy, whom I mentioned just now, was a very brave knight, but he was never looked upon as wise, either with regard to God, or to this world, as appears from the fact already related. Wherefore the great King Philip, when he was told that Count John of Chalons had a son, and that he was named Hugh, after the Duke of Burgundy, replied that he prayed God to make him a *preu homme*, like the duke, whose name he bore. They asked him why he had not said *prud' homme*, and he answered, "Because there is a great difference between *preu homme* and *prud' homme*, for there is many a *preu homme* knight in the lands both of Christians and Saracens, who never believed in God or His mother. Wherefore I say to you," he continued, "that God vouchsafes a great boon and grace to the Christian knight, whom He permits to be valiant in body, and whom He suffers to remain in His service, by preserving him from deadly sin. Whoso thus rules himself, deserves to be called *prud' homme*, because this prowess comes to him from God's bounteousness. While those of whom I spoke just now may he called *preux hommes*, because they are valiant in body, but do not fear either God or sin."

As for the great sums of money which the king expended in fortifying Jaffa, it is not expedient to speak of them, for they were beyond all reckoning, for he fortified the town from one shore to the other with twenty-four towers, and cleansed the ditches from mud without and within. There were three gates, one of which the legate built, together with a curtain of wall. To give you an idea of the expense the king incurred, I may tell you that I asked the legate how much this gate and this curtain had cost him. He asked me how much I thought. And I reckoned that the gate which he had built must have cost him 500 *livres*, and the curtain of wall 300. But he assured me, calling God to witness, that the gate and wall together had cost him fully 30,000 *livres*.

CHAPTER XIII.

A S soon as the king had completed the fortifications of the town of Jaffa, he took the resolution to go and reconstruct the fortifications of Sayette, which had been levelled by the Saracens. He commenced his march thither on the fête day of the Apostles St. Peter and St. Paul (June 29th), and the king lay with his army before the castle of Assur, which was very strong. On that evening the king convoked his people, and said that if they were of the same opinion with himself, he would go and seize upon a city of the Saracens called Naplous, named in the sacred writings Samaria. The Templars and Hospitallers unanimously answered that it was right to attempt to take the city, but they advised that he should not go in person, because if anything happened to him, the whole land would be lost. But he said that he would not allow them to go unless he went with them in person, and this enterprise was thus given up because the lords of the country would not consent that he should share in it. March after march, we came at last to the sands of Acre, where the king and army encamped. In this place there came to me a large party of men from Upper Armenia, who were going on pilgrimage to Jerusalem, by paying a heavy tribute to the Saracens who conducted them, with a dragoman who understood both their language and ours. They begged of me to let them see the sainted king. I went to where the king was seated in a tent, leaning against the tent pole, sitting on the sand, without a mat or anything else under him. I said to him, "Sire, there is without a great crowd from Armenia on their way to Jerusalem; and they entreat me, sire, to let them see the sainted king; but I have no desire just yet to kiss your bones." He laughed aloud, and told me to bring them in, and I did so. And when they had seen the king, they commended him to God, and the king did the same by them. On the morrow the army lay in a place called Passe-Poulain, where there is excellent water with which they irrigate the plant whence sugar is obtained.

While we were encamped there, one of my knights said to me: "Sir, I have lodged you better than you were yesterday."

Another knight, who had selected the previous spot, being greatly exasperated, sprang at him, and exclaimed: "You are very presumptuous to speak of anything I do." And he sprang upon him and seized him by the hair.

Thereupon I rushed at him, and struck him with my fist between the shoulders, and he let go his hold.

And I cried to him, "Quick, out of my house! For, so help me God, you shall never more be with me."

The knight went away displaying great grief, and brought to me Monseigneur Giles le Brun, constable of France, who, by reason of the sorrow evinced by the knight for the folly he had committed, besought me, as earnestly as he could, to take him back into my service.

But I replied that I would not take him back unless the legate would release me from my oath. Then they went to the legate, and related to him the circumstances; but the legate made answer that he had no power to release me, because the oath was a reasonable one, for the knight had well deserved it. I tell you all this, to put you on your guard against taking oaths, which it is wiser not to take, "for," says the wise man, "whoso swears easily, perjures himself easily."

On the next day the king went and encamped against the city of Sur, which is called Tyre in the Bible. There he convoked all the chief men of the army, and asked them if it would be advisable that he should take the town of Belinas, before he went to Sayette. We were unanimously of opinion that it was good that the king should send his people against it, but no one counselled that he should go in person, and with difficulty he was diverted from it. It was finally resolved that the Count of Eu should go, together with Monseigneur Philip de Montfort, the Sire de Sur, Monseigneur Giles le Brun, constable of France, Monseigneur Peter the Chamberlain, the Master of the Temple, and his community, the Master of the Hospital, and his community, and his brother likewise. We armed ourselves towards nightfall, and reached, a little after daybreak, a plain which lies before the town now called Belinas, but named in the Holy Scriptures Cæsarea Philippi. In this city a spring of water issues forth, called Jor; and in the midst of the plains stretching before the city is another beautiful spring, called Dan. And it happens that when the two streams from these springs join one another, they take the name of the river Jordan, wherein God was baptized.

With the consent of the Templars, the Count of Eu,

the Hospitallers, and the barons of the country who were there, it was arranged that the king's battle (in which I was then serving, because the king had retained the forty knights who were in my corps, and Monseigneur Geoffrey de Sargines likewise), should pass between the castle and the town, and that the barons of the country should enter the town on the left, and the Hospitallers on the right, and that the Templars should march straight in by the road on which we were then marching. We then put ourselves in motion until we came close to the town, when we discovered that the Saracens of the place had discomfited the king's sergeants, and driven them back. When I saw that, I went to the wise counsellors who were with the Count of Eu, and said to them: "Sirs, if you do not go where we are under orders to go, between the town and the castle, the Saracens will cut off our people who have entered the place." It was a perilous path to take, for the post for which we had been selected was the most perilous of all, for there were three sets of loose stone walls to cross, and the acclivity was so steep that a horse could hardly keep his feet, while the hill we were climbing was crowned on the top with a large array of mounted Turks. While I was speaking to them, I observed that our foot sergeants were pulling down the walls. When I noticed that, I said to those to whom I was speaking, that our orders were that the king's battle should go where the Turks then were, and that, for my part, since it had been so commanded, I should go. I and two of my knights then proceeded towards those who were pulling down the walls, and I saw a mounted sergeant try to pass over the wall, but his horse fell over upon him. Seeing that, I dismounted and led my horse by the bridle. When the Turks perceived us close at hand, as God willed, they abandoned to us the position at which we were aiming. From this spot a precipitous rock descended into the town. As soon as we got there, and the Turks had withdrawn, the Saracens who were in the town lost heart, and gave up the town to our people without a struggle. While I was there, the Marshal of the Temple was informed that I was in danger, and immediately began to ascend towards me. Also while I was there, the Germans who were in the Count of Eu's battle came up after me, and when they saw the Turks on horseback fleeing towards the castle, they prepared to pursue them. I said to them, "Sirs, you are wrong to do so, for we are where we were told to be, and you are going beyond our orders."

The castle which is above the town is called Subeyt, and is fully half a league up the mountains of Libanus, and the acclivity which goes up to the castle is scattered all over with rocks as big as meal tubs. When the Germans perceived that they were pursuing to no purpose, they turned to come back. Then the Saracens assailed them on foot, and dealt them, from the top of the rocks, weighty blows with their maces, and tore away the trappings of their horses. When our sergeants, who were with us, saw the mischance, they began to take fright; but I told them if they went away I would have them struck off the king's service for ever.

And they replied, "Sir, the stakes are not equal between us, for you are on horseback, and will gallop off, while we are on foot, and the Saracens will cut us to pieces."

I said to them, "Sirs, I promise you that I will not gallop off, for I will remain on foot beside you."

I dismounted, and sent my horse to the Templars, who were a good crossbow-shot in the rear. While the Germans were retreating, the Saracens struck with a bolt one of my knights in the throat, named Monseigneur John de Bussey, and he fell down dead before me.

Monseigneur Hugh d'Escoz, whose nephew he was, and who greatly distinguished himself in the Holy Land, said to me, " Sir, come and help us to carry my nephew below."

" Woe to him who helps you !" I exclaimed, " for you went up there contrary to orders. If evil has befallen you, it is your own fault. Carry him down to the dead-house, for I shall not move from this until they send to relieve me."

When Monseigneur John de Valenciennes heard of the danger we were in, he went to Monseigneur Oliver de Termes, and other chief men of Languedoc, and said to them, "Sirs, I pray and command you, in the king's name, to aid me in rescuing the seneschal."

While he was thus filled with anxiety, Monseigneur William de Beaumont came to him and said, " You are toiling for nothing, for the seneschal is dead."

But he replied, "Dead or alive, I will obtain tidings of him for the king."

Then he set out and came towards us where we were up in the mountain, and as soon as he had got up to us, he sent me word to come to him, and I did so.

Then Oliver de Termes told me that we were in great peril, for if we descended by the way we had ascended, we could not do it without great risk, because the declivity was so steep, and the Saracens could come down upon us, " but if you will follow my advise, I will deliver you without loss."

I asked him to explain what he wished, and I would do it.

"I will tell you," said he, "how we may escape. We will go along the top of this ridge, as if we were going towards Damascus, and the Saracens who are there will fancy that we mean to take them in the rear, and as soon as we have reached those plains we will push on round the city, and we shall be on the other side of the river before they can come after us. And at the same time we will work them much damage, for we will set fire to the threshed corn that is in the middle of those fields." We did as he pointed out, and took reeds like those of which flutes are made, and put live coal inside, and stuck them into the heaps of thrashed corn. And thus God brought us back in safety, thanks to Oliver de Termes' advice. And when we reached the camp where our people were, we found them all disarmed, for no one had given a thought to us On the morrow we returned to Sayette, where the king was.

We found that the king in person had superintended the interment of the bodies of the Christians, whom the Saracens had slaughtered, as I before related, and that he himself bore the putrid bodies, exhaling a terrible stench, to bury them in trenches, without stopping his nostrils, though the others stopped theirs. He procured labourers from all parts, and set about fortifying the city with lofty walls. and great towers; and when we came to the camp we found that he had measured our places, himself in person, where we were to lodge. My place be marked close to that of the Count of Eu, because he knew that the count liked my company.

I will tell you of the tricks the Count of Eu used to play us. I had erected a house where I and my knights used to take our meals with the door open. Now the door was facing the Count of Eu's tent, and he, being an excellent shot, made a small engine with which he fired into my house: and he used to watch when we were seated at table, and prepared his engine according to the length of our table, and broke our jars and glasses.

I had laid in a supply of hens and capons, and somebody had given him a young goose,[1] which he allowed to go with my hens, and it killed a dozen of them before we got there; and the woman who looked after them beat the goose with her petticoat.

While the king was fortifying Sayette merchants came to the camp who related to us how the Khan of the Tartars had taken the city of Bagdad and the Saracens' Pope, who was lord of the city, and styled the Caliph of Bagdad. The merchants described to us the manner in which the city and caliph were taken; after the king had laid siege to the city, the king sent to the caliph to say that he would gladly conclude a marriage between their children, and the caliph's counsellors were of opinion that he should consent to the alliance. Then the King of the Tartars required that he should send to him forty of his counsellors and greatest personages to confirm the marriage; and the caliph did so. The King of the Tartars then required of him a second time to send him forty of the noblest and richest men he had; and the caliph did so. And a third time he bade him send forty of the best men he had; and he did so. When the King of the Tartars saw that he had all the principal men of the city in his power, he judged that the common people would not defend themselves without leaders. He therefore cut off the heads of the hundred and

---

[1] One edition has *ourse* instead of *oue*, and is probably correct, a young bear being more likely to destroy the chickens than a young goose.

twenty men, and then carried the city by assault, and captured the caliph also.

To cover his breach of faith and to throw upon the caliph the blame of the capture of the city, he took the caliph and put him in an iron cage, and made him fast as long as a man can fast without dying, and then asked him if he were hungry. The caliph answered, " Yes ;" and no wonder.

Then the King of the Tartars ordered a large gold platter filled with precious stones to be brought, and said to him, " Dost thou know these jewels ?"

The caliph replied, " Yes, they were mine."

And he asked him if he was fond of them ? and the other said, " Yes."

" Since thou art fond of them," continued the King of the Tartars, " take as many of them as you please and eat them."

The caliph replied that he could not, " For it was not the sort of food anyone could eat."

Thereupon the King of the Tartars said to him, " Thou seest on this platter thy means of defence ; for if thou hadst given thy treasure of gold thou couldst have defended thyself successfully against us, by spending this treasure which now fails thee in the greatest need thou ever hadst."

While the king was fortifying Sayette I went one day to mass at the break of day, and he bade me wait for him, because he was going to ride out, and I did so. When we were in the fields we came opposite to a small church, and while on horseback we saw a priest chanting the mass. The king told me that this church was built in honour of the miracle which God wrought in expelling the devil from the body of the widow's daughter ; and he said that, if I pleased, he would hear the mass

which the priest had begun; and I said that it seemed
to me a right thing to do. When they came to the
part where the *pax* is offered, I observed that the clerk
who was intoning the mass was tall, swarthy, lean, and
with bristling hair; and the fear seized me, that if he
bore the *pax* to the king he might perhaps be an as-
sassin, a bad man, and might perhaps kill the king.
I went therefore and took the *pax* from the clerk, and
carried it to the king. When the mass was chanted
and we had mounted our horses we saw the legate in
the fields, and the king went up to him, and called me,
and said to the legate, " I complain to you of the
seneschal, for handing me the *pax*; and not allowing
the poor clerk to offer it."

Then I told the legate the reason why I had done so;
and the legate said I did what was right. But the king
replied, " Truly, no!" Thereupon a great discussion
arose between them, in consequence of which I was left
in peace. And I have related to you this story that
you might remark his great humility.

The miracle which God worked upon the widow's
daughter is described in the Gospel, which says that
when God performed it He was *in parte Tyri et Sidonis;*
for in those days the city which I call Sur was Tyre,
and the city which I have hitherto named Sayette was
Sidon.

While the king was fortifying Sayette, there came to
him messengers from a great lord from the further end
of Greece, who called himself the great Comnenus and
Sire of Trebizond. They brought to the king various
curiosities as a present; among others, bows of horn, the
bolts of which were inserted in the bows by means of
screws, and when they were discharged they issued forth
very sharp-pointed and well made. They asked the king

to send a princess of his palace to their lord, that he might take her to be his wife. And the king replied, that he had not brought any from beyond sea, and advised them to go to the emperor at Constantinople, who was his cousin, and beg him to give them for their lord a wife of the king's and his own lineage. The king did that in order that the emperor might make an alliance with this great and rich lord against Vataces, who was then emperor of the Greeks.

The queen, who had just recovered from the birth of Madame Blanche, of whom she was confined at Jaffa, arrived at Sayette, for she had come by sea. When I heard that she had arrived, I rose up from before the king and went to meet her, and conducted her to the castle. And when I returned to the king, who was in his chapel, he asked me if the queen and the children were well; and I answered, " Yes."

And he said to me, " I knew quite well, when you rose up from before me, that you were going to meet the queen, and therefore I stayed for the sermon."

I recall all these things because, during the five years I had been with him, he had never, so far as I know, spoken of the queen or his children either to myself or to anyone else; and it was not a good practice, as I thought, to be a stranger to his own wife and children.

CHAPTER XIV.

N All Saints' Day I invited to my house, which was on the shore, all the rich men in the camp; and just then a poor knight arrived in a boat with his wife and four boys. I made them come and eat in my house. When we had eaten, I spoke to the rich men who were there, and said to them, " Let us give large alms and relieve this poor man of his children; let each take one, and I will take one." Each took one, and disputed among themselves who should have one. When the poor knight saw that, he and his wife began to weep for joy. It happened that when the Count of Eu returned from the king's quarters, where he had dined, he came to see the men of quality who were with me, and took from me my boy, who was about twelve years' old, and who served the count so faithfully and well, that after we returned to France he married him and made him a knight. And whenever I came to where the count lived he would hardly quit me, and used to say, " Sir, God reward you! for it was you who brought me to the honour I enjoy." As for the three other brothers, I know not what became of them.

I entreated the king to allow me to go on a pilgrimage to Nòtre Dame de Tortosa, which was a great resort of pilgrims, because the first altar that was ever built in honour of the Mother of God upon earth was there. And Our Lady wrought there many great miracles; and among others there was one possessed, who had a devil in his body; when his friends, who brought him there were praying to the Mother of God to restore him to health, the enemy who was within him replied, " Our Lady is not here, but in Egypt to aid the King of France and the Christians, who will this day land on foot in the face of the unbelievers on horseback." The day was marked down in writing, and was shown to the legate, for monseigneur told me so with his own lips. And it is certain that she did aid us, and would have aided us still further had we not offended her, and her Son, as I have before related.

The king gave me leave to go there, and desired me, in full council, to buy him a hundred pieces of camlet of different colours, to bestow upon the Franciscans when we returned to France. Then my heart grew calm, for I judged that he would not stay much longer. When we reached Tripoli, my knights asked me what I proposed to do with the camlet, and begged me to tell them. " Perhaps," said I, " I stole it to make money by it."

The Prince of Tripoli (whom may God absolve!) made as much rejoicing and showed us as much honour as he could; and would have bestowed rich gifts upon myself and my knights if we would have taken anything. But we declined to accept anything except relics, which I took back to the king, together with the pieces of camlet which I had purchased for him.

Besides, I sent four pieces of camlet to the queen, The knight who took them carried them wrapt in a

x

white cloth. When the queen saw him enter the room where she was, she knelt down before him, and the knight knelt down in his turn before her; and the queen said to him, " Rise, sir knight; you, the bearer of relics, ought not to kneel down."

But the knight replied, " Madam, these are not relics, but pieces of camlet which my lord sends to you."

When the queen heard that, she and her maidens began to laugh, and the queen said to my knight, " Tell your lord that I wish bad luck to him for making me kneel before his camlet."

While the king was at Sayette they brought him a stone which was formed in layers, the most wonderful thing in the world; for when a layer was raised there was seen, between the two stones, the figure of a sea-fish. The fish was of stone, but there was nothing wanting to its form, neither eyes, nor bones, nor colour, nor anything to mark a difference between what it was and what it would be if still alive. The king asked for a stone and found a tench within, of a brownish colour, and exactly what a tench ought to be.

At Sayette the king received tidings of the death of his mother. He manifested such great grief thereat, that for two days nobody could speak to him. After that he sent a serving-man for me. When I stood before him in his chamber, where he was all alone, and as soon as he saw me he opened his arms and cried, " Ah! Seneschal, I have lost my mother!"

" Sire, I am not surprised at that," I replied; " for she could not avoid dying; but I am surprised that you, who are a man of sense, should have displayed so much sorrow, for you know that the wise man has said, ' That whatever grief a man may have at his heart, nothing ought to appear on his countenance; for whoso does this, renders his enemies joyful and disappoints his friends.'"

He caused many fine services to be performed for her beyond the sea, and afterwards he sent to France a ship charged with letters of supplication to the churches that they would pray for her.

Madam Marie de Vertus, a very excellent and pious lady, came to inform me that the queen displayed great affliction, and begged me to go to her and comfort her. When I came to her I found her weeping, and I said to her that he spoke the truth who declared that no faith was to be put in woman; " for she was the woman you hated above all others, and yet you show all this sorrow for her." She replied that it was not for the queen she wept, but for what the king suffered in mourning for her, and also for her daughter (afterwards Queen of Navarre) who was left to the care of men.

So great was the harshness Queen Blanche exhibited towards Queen Margaret that, so far as she could, she would never allow her son to be in his wife's company, except at night, when he went to lie with her. The palace, where they best liked to stay, was at Pontoise, because the king's chamber was above and the queen's chamber below. And they had so well contrived their affairs that they held their interviews on a winding staircase which went from one chamber to the other; and they had so arranged that when the ushers saw the queen coming to the chamber of the king, her son, they knocked at the door with their wands, and the king ran down to his chamber, that his mother might find him there; and in like manner did the ushers at the door of Queen Margaret's chamber, when the Queen Blanche was coming, so that she might find Queen Margaret there. On one occasion the king was standing by the side of the queen, his wife, when she was in great danger of her life, for she had grievously suffered from the birth of a child.

Queen Blanche came then and took her son by the hand, and said to him, " Come away, you can do nothing here."

When Queen Margaret saw that his mother was taking the king away, she cried out, " Alas! you will not let me, dead or living, see my husband." And then she swooned away, and it was thought she was dead; and the king, believing she was dead, came back, and with great difficulty she was restored to consciousness.

When the fortifications of the city of Sayette were nearly completed, the king caused several processions to be made throughout the camp, and on the termination of the processions he asked the legate to pray that God would order the king's affairs· according to His will so that he should do what was most pleasing unto God, whether by returning to France or by remaining there.

After the processions were ended, the king, at a time when I was seated with the rich men of the country, called me into an enclosure and made me turn my back to them. Then the legate said to me :—

" Seneschal, the king has a very high sense of your services, and will very gladly procure you profit and honour; and to put your heart at ease, he has desired me to tell you that he has arranged his affairs to return to France at the ensuing Easter."

I replied: " God grant he may achieve his desire!"

Then the legate bade me accompany him to his house, where he shut me and himself into a small room, where there was no one else present, and put my two hands within his own and began to shed many tears; and when he could speak, he said to me :—

" Seneschal, I am very happy, and render thanks unto God for that the king and the other pilgrims have escaped from the great peril you have encountered in this land; and I am grieved at heart that I must leave your blessed company and go to the court of Rome, to be among the unfaithful who are there. But I will tell you what I think of doing. I think of so managing it that I may remain here a year after you, for I desire to expend all my money in fortifying the suburbs of Acre, in order to show them very clearly that I do not take any money away with me; they will not then run after a man whose hands are empty."

I once mentioned to the legate two sins that one of my priests had related to me, and he replied to me after this manner: " No one knows so well as I do the sins of unfaithfulness that are committed in Acre, wherefore God will avenge them in such fashion that the city will be cleansed in the blood of its inhabitants, and another people will come who shall inhabit it after that." The prophecy of the worthy man already is verified in part, for the city has been washed in the blood of its inhabitants; but they who ought to inhabit it have not yet come; and God grant that they may be worthy of it, according to His good pleasure.

After all this, the king bade me arm myself and my knights. I asked him for what purpose, and he said that it was to escort the queen and his children to Sur, which was fully seven leagues distant. I made no reply, though the service was a very perilous one, for we had neither peace nor truce either with those of Egypt or those of Damascus. By God's mercy, we arrived there in peace, without let or hindrance, and at nightfall, although we had twice been obliged to dismount on the land of our enemies, to kindle a fire and cook food, to nourish and give milk to the infants.

When the king departed from the city of Sayette, which he had fortified with great walls and towers, and with broad moats cleaned within and without, the patriarchs and barons of the country came and addressed him in this wise :—

" Sire, you have fortified the city of Sayette, and that of Cæsarea, and the town of Jaffa, all of which is a great advantage for the Holy Land; and you have greatly strengthened Acre by the walls and towers you have built.   Sire, we have deliberated among ourselves, and we do not see that your sojourn here can be of any benefit to the kingdom of Jerusalem; wherefore we advise and counsel you to proceed to Acre in the coming Lent, and to prepare your passage so that you may return to France after Easter."

By the advice of the patriarch and barons, the king quitted Sayette and proceeded to Sur, where the queen was; and from there we came to Acre at the beginning of Lent.

During the whole of Lent the king fitted out his ships to return to France; there were thirteen of them, ships and galleys.   These were got ready so that the king and queen embarked on St. Mark's eve (April 24th, 1254) after Easter, and we had a fair wind on setting out.   On St. Mark's day the king told me that it was on that day he was born; and I remarked that he might say that he was born a second time, now that he had escaped from that land of peril.

On Saturday we sighted the island of Cyprus, and a mountain in the island which is called the Mountain of the Cross.   On that day a fog arose, and descended from the land upon the sea, so that our mariners fancied that we were farther from Cyprus than we really were, because they saw the mountain above the fog.

They therefore advanced boldly, whence it happened that our ship struck against a bank of sand which was covered with water : and had not we struck against this bank of sand, we should have driven right on to a mass of rocks that were hidden, where our ship would have been shattered, and ourselves wrecked and drowned. Immediately cries resounded through the vessel, and everyone exclaimed, " Alas ! " and the mariners and others wrung their hands, because everyone feared they would all be drowned. On hearing this I rose from my bed whereon I was lying, and went to the castle with the sailors. When I came there brother Remon, who was a Templar and master of the mariners, said to one of his servants : " Cast the lead ! " and he did so. And, as soon as he had cast it, he exclaimed : " Alas ! we are aground." When brother Remon heard that he tore his robe to his girdle, and began to pluck out his beard and to cry aloud : " Alas ! alas ! " At that moment one of my knights, named Monseigneur John de Monson, father of the Abbot William of St. Michael's, showed a great kindness to me in this, that, without saying a word to me, he brought me a surcoat, lined, and threw it over my back, because I had only my coat on. I called out to him and said :—

" What am I to do with the surcoat you bring me, when we are drowning ? "

He answered : " Upon my soul, sir, I would rather that we were all drowned than that you should catch through the cold a disease of which you would have to die."

The sailors shouted out : " Galley, a-hoy ! to take the king on board ! " But of four galleys that the king had there not one drew near, in which they acted very wisely, for there were 800 persons in the ship, all of whom would have sprung into the galleys to save their lives, and would have sent them all to the bottom.

The man who had cast the lead cast it a second time, and went to brother Remon and told him that the ship was no longer upon the shoal. Then brother Remon went to the king, who was stretched crosswise on the deck, barefooted, clad in a simple tunic, and his hair in disorder (before the body of our Lord, which was in the ship), like a man who had made up his mind to be drowned.

As soon as it was day, we saw right ahead the rock against which we should have been driven if the ship had not struck upon the bank of sand.

In the morning the king sent for the sailing-master of the fleet, who ordered four divers to go down to the bottom of the sea ; and they plunged in, and when they came up again, the king and the sailing-master heard them one after the other, so that no one of the divers knew what the others had said ; however, it was ascertained from the four divers that our ship in grating against the sand had lost three fathoms of the keel upon which she was constructed.

Then the king summoned the sailing-masters before us, and asked them what advice they would give touching the shock his ship had received. They consulted together, and counselled the king to leave the ship he was in and go on board another. "And we give you this counsel because we believe for certain that all the planking of your ship is loosened ; wherefore we fear that when your ship is out at sea she will not be able to sustain the shock of the waves, and will go to pieces. For it happened in the same manner when we came from France that a ship took the ground, and when it put out to sea it could not withstand the buffeting of the waves, but broke up, and all who were on board perished except a woman and a child, who escaped on a fragment of the wreck."

I can bear witness that they spoke the truth, for I saw in the household of Count de Joigny, in the city of Paphos, the woman and child, whom the count supported.

The king then asked Monseigneur Peter the Chamberlain, Monseigneur Giles le Brun, Constable of France, Monseigneur Gervais d'Escraines, the king's head cook, the Archdeacon of Nicosin, who bore his seal, and was afterwards a cardinal, and myself, what we recommended him to do in these circumstances. And we all replied that in every circumstance of life it was wise to trust to those who had the best knowledge of the subject: " We therefore counsel you, so far as it lies with us, to do what the sailing-masters advise."

Then the king said to the sailing-masters, " I ask of you, upon your honour, supposing the ship were yours, and it were laden with merchandize, would you abandon her ? "

And they all answered, " No," because they would rather run the hazard of being drowned than give upwards of 4000 *livres* for a ship.

" Why, then, do you advise me to leave the ship ?"

" Because," said they, " it is not at all the same thing; for neither silver nor gold would be equivalent to the worth of your life, and of the lives of your wife and children who are on board; and for that reason we do not advise you to put yourself or them into danger."

The king then said, " Sirs, I have heard your opinion and that of my own people; and now in my turn I will tell you mine, which is that, if I leave the ship, there are upwards of 500 persons on board who will remain in the island of Cyprus, from fear of peril to their person, (for there is not one of them who does not love his life as much as I do mine), and who, peradventure, will never return to their country. For which reason I prefer to entrust to God's keeping my own life and the lives of my wife and children, rather than cause so much hurt to such a large number of persons as are on board."

The great inconvenience the king would have caused to the people in his ship may be seen from the example of Oliver de Termes, who was in the king's ship. He was one of the bravest men I ever saw, and one of those who most distinguished themselves in the Holy Land; but he dared not remain with us, for fear of being drowned. So he stayed behind in Cyprus, and a year and a-half passed before he rejoined the king, though he was a great and wealthy man, and could well pay for his passage. Consider, then, what the common folk would have done who had not wherewithal to pay, when such a man met with so much difficulty.

Out of this peril, in which God had preserved us, we fell into another; for the wind which had carried us to Cyprus, where we were so nearly drowned, rose so strong and terrible that it drove us with violence upon the island; for the mariners threw out their anchors against the wind, but could not bring the ship up until they had let go five. It became necessary to break down the bulk-heads of the king's cabin, and no one dared remain in it for fear of being blown into the sea by the wind. At that moment, while the Constable of France, Monseigneur Giles le Brun, and myself, were lying down in the king's cabin, the queen opened the door, thinking to find the king there. I asked what she had come to seek; and she told me that she had come to speak to the king, to pray him to vow unto God or His saints a pilgrimage,

for which God should deliver us out of the danger we
were in; for the mariners had told us that we were in
danger of being drowned. And I said to her, " Madam,
vow a pilgrimage to Monseigneur St. Nicholas de Va-
rangeville, and I will answer for him that God shall
bring you to France—you, the king, and your children."

" Seneschal," she replied, " in sooth, I would gladly
do so; but the king is so odd, that if he knew I had
vowed it without him, he would never permit me to go."

" You shall do this, then : if God will lead you back
to France, you shall vow unto him a ship of silver of
the value of five marks, for the king, yourself, and your
three children; and I guarantee to you that God will
bring you back to France; for I have vowed unto St.
Nicholas that if he rescued us from the danger we have
been in this night, I will go to pray at his shrine from
Joinville on foot and without shoon."

Then she said that for the ship of silver of the value
of five marks she made the vow unto St. Nicholas, and
she added that I must pledge myself for him. And I
answered, that I would do so readily. She then went
away, but only for a little space, for she presently returned and said, " St. Nicholas has preserved us from
this peril; for the wind has gone down."

After the queen (whom may God absolve!) got back
to France, she had a ship made of silver at Paris; and
on board were the king, the queen, and the three
children, all of silver; the mariner, the mast, the helm,
and the rigging, all of silver; and the sails all of silver;
and the queen told me that the fashioning of it had cost
a hundred livres. When the ship was finished, the queen
sent it to me at Joinville that I might take it to St.
Nicholas's, and I did so. And I saw it was still at St.

Nicholas's when we conducted the king's sister[1] to Haguenau, to the king of Germany.

Let us return now to our subject, and tell how after we had escaped from these two perils, the king seated himself on the bulwark of the ship and made me sit down at his feet, and said, " Seneschal, our God has clearly shown to us his great power; for one of these little winds (not the chief of the four winds) has very nearly drowned the king of France, his wife and children, and all his company; we ought, therefore, to be grateful to Him, and render thanks unto Him for the peril out of which He has delivered us."

" Seneschal," continued the king, " when such tribulations, or grievous sicknesses, or other afflictions, befall individuals, holy men say that these are our Lord's threatenings; for in like manner, as God says to those who recover from grievous sicknesses, ' You see now that I could have made you die, had I willed it.' So can He say to us, ' You see that I could have drowned you, had I willed it.' We ought, therefore," said the king, " to look into ourselves, lest there be anything in us that displeases Him, in order to put it away from us; for if we act otherwise after this warning He has sent us, He will smite us with death, or some other great calamity, to the hurt of our souls and bodies."

The king observed: " Seneschal, the holy man says, ' Lord God, why dost Thou threaten us? For if Thou hadst cast us all away, Thou wouldst not for that be the poorer; and if Thou hadst saved us all, Thou wouldst not for that be the richer. Whence we may perceive,' remarks the holy man, ' that the threatenings which God

---

[1] The Princess Blanche, sister of Philip the Fair, married to Rodolph, son of Albert, Emperor of Germany, A.D. 1300.

addresses to us are not sent for His benefit, or to turn
aside His loss, but solely because of the great love He
has for us. He awakens us by His threatenings, that we
may clearly see our faults, and that we may pluck out
what is displeasing to Him.' Let us, therefore," said
the king, " act thus, and we shall do wisely."

We sailed from Cyprus, after we had taken in fresh
water and other supplies of which we stood in need.
We came to an island called Lampedusa, where we
found swarms of rabbits, and an ancient hermitage in
the rocks, and gardens made there by the hermits, who,
in past times, had died there; and there were olive-
bushes and fig-trees, and vines, and other trees. A
stream from a spring flowed through the garden. The
king and the rest of us went to the end of the garden,
and under the first vault we found an oratory whitened
with lime, and a red cross of earth. We passed under
a second vault, and there discovered two dead bodies,
the flesh of which had withered away; the ribs still
held together, and the bones of the hands were upon
their breasts, and they were lying towards the east, in
the same direction as bodies buried in the ground. As
we were re-embarking on board our ship, one of our
mariners was missed, wherefore the master of the ship
judged that he had remained behind to turn hermit, and
on that account Nicholas de Soisi, the king's master-
sergeant, left three bags of biscuits on the shore, that
he might find and subsist on them.

When we had sailed from there, we saw a great
island in the sea, called Pantalarea, peopled with Saracens, who were subject to the King of Sicily and the
King of Tunis. The queen begged the king to send
three galleys to procure some fruit for his children.
The king consented, and commanded the galleys to be

ready to come off to him when his ship passed by the island. The galleys entered the island by means of a creek, but when the king's ship came off the creek, we heard no news of our galleys. Then the mariners began to speak in a low voice among themselves, and the king called them to him, and asked them what they thought of this adventure. And the mariners told him that the Saracens had taken his people and galleys.

"But we counsel and advise you, sire, not to wait for them, for you are between the kingdom of Sicily and the kingdom of Tunis, neither of which bears you much love, and if you will let us set sail, we shall have delivered you out of danger before the night is over, for we shall have passed through this strait."

"Truly," answered the king, "I will not take your advice to leave my people in the hands of the Saracens until I have done all in my power to recover them. And I command you to turn your sails so that we may bear down towards them."

When the queen heard that, she began to afflict herself grievously, and cried aloud, "Alas! it is I who am the cause of all this."

While they were turning the sails of the king's ship, and of the others, we saw the galleys standing out from the island. When they came near, the king asked the mariners why they had acted in this manner, and they replied that they could not help themselves, for they who were to blame were sons of Parisian burgesses, six in number, who would eat of the fruit of the gardens, wherefore they could not bring them off, and yet were unwilling to leave them behind. Then the king commanded that they should be put into the boat astern, whereupon they began to cry and sob. "Sire, for

God's sake ransom us at the price of all we possess, but do not put us where robbers and murderers are put, for that would be a reproach to us for ever." The queen and the rest of us did all we could to induce the king to relent; but he refused to listen to anyone, and they were put there, and left there, till we reached the land. They were in such danger, that when the sea was rough the waves dashed over their heads, and they were obliged to sit down lest the wind should blow them into the sea. And this was only just, for their gluttony worked us so much hurt, that we were delayed fully a week, because the king had the ships turned completely round.

Before we came to land, another adventure befell us at sea after this manner. One of the queen's tiring women, after she had put the queen to bed, took no heed, but threw the stuff which she had wound round her head close to the iron stove where the queen's candle was burning. And when she had gone to lie down in the cabin below the queen's, where the women slept, the candle burnt down until the flame caught the stuff, and from the stuff caught the cloth with which the queen's sheets were covered. When the queen awoke, she saw the cabin filled with flames, and jumped out of bed all naked, and seizing the stuff, threw it into the sea, and took the sheets and extinguished them. Those who were in the skiff cried out in stifled tones, "Fire! Fire!" I raised my head, and saw the stuff still burning, with a clear flame upon the sea, which was very calm. I put on my coat as quickly as I could, and went and sat down with the mariners. While I was sitting there, my squire, who slept in front of me, came to me and said that the king was awake, and had asked where I was.

"And I answered him," said he, "that you were in the cabin.   And the king replied, ' thou liest.' "

While we were talking, Master Geoffrey, the queen's clerk, came up to me and said, " Be not alarmed, for it happened in this wise."

And I said to him, " Master Geoffrey, go and tell the queen that the king is awake, and beg her to go and quiet him."

On the morrow the Constable of France, and Monseigneur Peter, the Chamberlain, and Monseigneur Gervaise, said to the king: "What happened last night, that we heard a cry of fire?"   I said never a word.   Then the king answered, " It must have been very bad, since the seneschal is more guarded about it than I am.   But I will tell you," he continued, " what it was, and how we all missed being burnt to death last night."   And he told them how it all happened, and then said to me, " Seneschal, I command you from this time never to retire to rest until you have put out all the fires on board, except the great fire which is in the hold of the ship.   And know that I shall not myself lie down until you have come back to me."   And I did so as long as we were at sea; and when I came back to the king he laid down for the night.

Another adventure befell us at sea, for Monseigneur Dragonet, a rich man of Provence was sleeping in the morning in his ship, which was a good league ahead of ours, and he called to his squire and said to him, " Go and close me that window, for the sun strikes on my face."   The other saw that he could not close the window without going outside the ship, so he went outside.   But while he was going to close the window, his foot slipped, and he fell into the sea; and this ship had no boat astern, for it was a small vessel.   Very soon the ship was far away. We who were in the king's vessel thought it was a parcel, or cask, for he who fell into the water showed no resolution. One of the king's galleys picked him up, and brought him to our ship, where he told us what had happened to him. I asked him how it was that he showed no resolution to save himself, either by swimming, or in any other way. He replied that there was no need or occasion for him to exhibit any resolution, for as soon as he felt that he was falling into the water, he committed himself to Our Lady, who supported him by the shoulders from the time he went overboard, until he was picked up by the king's galley. In honour of this miracle, I had the incident painted at Joinville, in my chapel, and on the glass before the relics at Blécourt.

After being six weeks at sea, we ran into a port about two leagues from the castle called Hyères, which belonged to the Count of Provence, who was afterwards King of Sicily. The queen and all the council were of opinion that the king should disembark there, because the land was his brother's. The king replied that he would not leave the ship until he reached Aigues-Mortes, which was in his own land. The king kept us thus all Wednesday and Thursday, so that we could not move him. In those Marseilles ships there are two rudders, which are attached to two tillers so ingeniously that, as quickly as you may guide a horse, you may direct the vessel to the right or left.

The king was seated on the Friday upon one of the tillers, and called me to him and said, "Seneschal, what do you think of this affair?"

And I answered, "Sire, it would be only just if it happened to you as it did to Madame de Bourbon, who would not alight in this port, but put out to

o

74

sea to go to Aigues-Mortes, and was seven weeks at sea."

Then the king summoned his council, and told them what I had said to him, and asked them what they would advise him to do, and all were of opinion that he ought to land, for that he would not act wisely if he placed his own person, and those of his wife and children, in venture upon the sea, after he was once out of it. The king yielded to the counsel we gave him, at which the queen was much rejoiced.

The king disembarked at the Château d'Hyères, as did also the queen, and his children. While the king was staying at Hyères, endeavouring to procure horses to take him into France, the Abbot of Cluny, who was afterwards Bishop of Olive, made him a present of two palfreys, which were worth fully 500 *livres*, one for himself, and one for the queen.

When he had made him this present, he said to the king, "Sire, I will come to you to-morrow, and speak of my affairs."

On the morrow the abbot returned, and the king listened to him very attentively, and for a long time.

When the abbot had taken leave, I went to the king and said to him, "I wish to ask you, if you please, if you have listened more graciously to the Abbot of Cluny, because he gave you, yesterday, those two palfreys."

The king reflected for some time, and then answered, "Truly, yes."

"Sire," I continued, "do you know why I put this question to you?"

"Why?" asked he.

"Sire," I answered, "because I counsel and advise you to forbid your sworn counsellors, when you come into France, to take anything from those who have causes to plead before you, for rest assured that if they receive anything, they will listen more patiently and attentively to those who give them something, as you have done by the Abbot of Cluny."

Then the king summoned his council, and repeated to them what I had said, and they replied that I had given him good advice.

The king had heard mention made of a Franciscan friar named brother Hugh, and because of the great reputation he had, he sent for him to hear him speak. The day he came to Hyères, we looked out over the road by which he was coming and observed that a great crowd of men and women followed him. The king bade him preach. The commencement of the sermon was upon monks, and he spoke after this manner. "Sirs," said he, "I see many monks at the king's court in his company." And after these words he continued. "I, the foremost, and I declare that they are not in a state to save themselves, or the Holy Scriptures lie unto us, which cannot be. For the Holy Scriptures tell us the monk cannot live out of his cloister without deadly sin, any more than a fish can live out of water. And if the monks who are with the king call that a cloister, I tell them it is the largest one I ever saw, for it extends from this side of the sea to the other. If they affirm that in this cloister it is possible to lead a self-denying life to save their soul, upon that point I do not believe them, especially after eating with them of a great quantity of different sorts of meat, and drinking wine good and strong. Wherefore I am certain, that if they had been in their cloister, they would not have been so comfortably off as they are with the king."

In his sermon he taught the king how he ought to

conduct himself if he would be loved by his people; and at the end of his sermon he said that he had read the Bible and the books that go along with the Bible; and that he had never seen, either in the book of the believers, or in those of the unbelievers, that any kingdom or lordship was ever lost, or passed from one lord to another or from one king to another, except from want of justice. "Let the king take heed, then," said he, "now that he is going into France, to do justice to his people, so that he may retain God's love, and that God may not wrest out of his hands the kingdom of France during his lifetime."

I spoke to the king not to let him quit his company so long as he could help it; but brother Hugh would do nothing to oblige the king.

Then the king took me by the hand and said, "Let us go again and ask him."

We went to him, and I said to him, "Sir, do what my lord asks of you, and tarry with him as long as he remains in Provence."

But he replied to me, angrily, "Certes, sir, I will not do so, but will go where it will be more pleasing unto God to behold me than in the company of the king"

He stayed one day with us, and on the morrow went away. I have been told that he is buried in the city of Marseilles, where he works many fine miracles.

On the day the king set out from Hyères, he went down from the castle on foot, because the hill was too steep, and he went so far upon foot that he was obliged to mount my palfrey, for he could not have his own. And when his palfrey had come up, he fell upon Ponce, the squire, and when he had soundly trounced him, I said, "Sire, you ought to make great allowance for Ponce, the squire, for he has served your grandfather, your father, and yourself."

"Seneschal," he replied, "he has not served us; but it is we who have served him, in suffering him to be near us with the bad qualities he possesses. For King Philip, my grandfather, told me that we ought to reward our people, some more, some less, according as they serve us; and he also said that no one could be a good ruler of the land if he knew not how to refuse, as well as how to give. And I tell you these things," said the king, "because this generation is so greedy in asking for favours, that there are few who look to the salvation of their souls, or the honour of their persons, provided they can draw to themselves their neighbours' goods, whether rightly or wrongly."

The king proceeded through the county of Provence until he came to a city called Aix-en-Provence, where, it is said, the body of the Magdalen is interred. We passed under a very lofty vault of rocks, where, it is said, the Magdalen lived in a hermitage for seventeen years. When the king arrived at Beaucaire, and I saw him on his own land, and in his own domain, I took leave of him, and went to visit my niece, the Dauphiness of Vienne, and my uncle, the Count of Châlons, and his son, the Count of Burgundy; and after I had stayed some time at Joinville, and had arranged my affairs, I returned to the king, whom I found at Soissons, and who, on my account, made such great rejoicings, that all who were there marvelled at it. I found there Count John of Brittany, and the daughter of King Thibaud, his wife, who offered to do homage to the king for all the rights and titles she possessed in Champagne; and the king cited her, as well as King Thibaud of Navarre, second of that name, to appear before the parliament which was held at Paris, to hear the parties, and do them justice.

The King of Navarre came before the parliament with his council, and likewise the Count of Brittany. At this parliament King Thibaud demanded in marriage Madame Isabelle, the king's daughter. Notwithstanding what our people of Champagne said of me behind my back, because of the love they had seen the king display towards me at Soissons, I did not the less go to the king at Paris to speak of that marriage. "Go," said the king, "make peace with the Count of Brittany, and then we will arrange our marriage." I observed to him that he ought not to give it up on that account. But he replied that for no consideration would he consent to the marriage until peace was made, so that it should not be said that he married his daughters by disinheriting his barons.

I reported these words to Queen Margaret of Navarre, and to the king, her son, and to their other counsellors, and when they heard that, they hastened to make peace. And after peace was made, the King of France gave his daughter to King Thibaud, and their nuptials were celebrated at Melun with grandeur and magnificence, and thence King Thibaud conducted her to Provins, into which he entered, attended by a great array of barons.

CHAPTER XV.

FTER the king's return from beyond sea, he lived so devoutly, that he never afterwards wore furs of different colours, or minnever, nor scarlet cloth, nor gilt stirrups or spurs; his dress was of camlet, and of a dark blue cloth; the linings of his coverlids and garments were of docskin or hares-legs.

When rich men's minstrels entered the hall, after the repast, bringing with them their viols, he waited to hear grace, until the minstrel had finished his chant, then he rose, and the priests who said grace stood before him. When we were at his court in a private way, he used to sit at the foot of his bed, and when the Franciscans and Dominicans who where there spoke of a book that would give him pleasure, he would say to them : " You shall not read to me, for, after eating, there is no book so pleasant as *quolibets,*" that is, that every one should say what he likes. When men of quality dined with him, he made himself agreeable to them.

I will speak to you now of his wisdom. Upon one occasion it was declared that there was no one in his council as wise as himself. And it appeared in this that of himself, without consulting anyone, and off-hand, as

I have heard, he replied to all the prelates of France, touching a request they made to him to this effect :—

Bishop Guy, of Auxerre, spoke to him in the name of all. "Sire," said he, "these archbishops and bishops who are here have commissioned me to tell you that Christianity is decaying and perishing in your hands, and that it will decay still further if you do not see to it, because no one now-a-days has any fear of an excommunication. We require of you, therefore, sire, that you command your bailiffs and sergeants that they constrain those who have been excommunicated for a year and a day to render satisfaction to the Church." And the king replied to them of himself, without consultation, that he would be quite willing to command his bailiffs and sergeants to constrain the excommunicated, as they requested of him, provided they would give him cognizance of the sentence, to decide if it were just or not. Then they consulted together, and answered the king that they would not give him cognizance of what belonged to the ecclesiastical court. The king thereupon replied in his turn that he would not give them cognizance of what belonged to himself, nor would he command his sergeants to constrain the excommunicated to seek absolution, whether they were in the right or in the wrong. "For, if I did so, I should act contrary to God's will and to justice. And I will give you, as an example, the Count of Brittany, whom the Bishops of Brittany kept for seven years under excommunication, when he obtained absolution from the court of Rome, and had I constrained him at the end of one year, I should have done so wrongfully."

It came to pass, after our return from beyond sea, that the monks of St. Urban's elected two abbots, both of whom Bishop Peter of Châlons (whom may God absolve!) expelled, and consecrated in their stead Monseigneur John de Mymeri, and conferred upon him the crozier. I refused to receive him, because he had done wrong to Abbot Geoffrey, who had appealed against him and gone to Rome. I kept the abbey in my own hands until Geoffrey should have gained the crozier, and the other lost it to whom it was given by the bishop, and so long as the dispute lasted the bishop caused me to be excommunicated. On this account a great quarrel arose at a parliament held at Paris between myself, the Bishop Peter of Flanders, the Countess Margaret of Flanders, and the Archbishop of Reims, whom she contradicted. At the next ensuing parliament all the prelates besought the king to come by himself and speak to them. When he returned from conferring with them he came up to us who were waiting for him in the antechamber of the palace, and told us laughingly of the squabbles he had had with the prelates. In the first place, the Archbishop of Reims had said to the king :—

"Sire, what compensation will you make me for the custody of St. Remy's relics at Reims, which you are taking out of my hands? For I would not have upon my conscience such a sin as you have committed for all the kingdom of France."

"By the relics which are here," exclaimed the king, "you would do as much for Compiegne, so great is the covetousness that is in you. Is there any perjury in that?"

"The Bishop of Chartres required of me," continued the king, "to restore to him what I kept back of his; and I told him I would not do so until what was due to me was paid. And I said to him that he had done me homage, his hands between mine, but that he did not conduct himself loyally and justly towards me when he sought to deprive me of my heritage. The Bishop of Chartres, said to me," pursued the king: "'Sire, what will you do for me with regard to the Seigneur de Joinville, who wrests from this poor monk the abbey of St. Urban?'"

"Sir Bishop," answered the king, "you have made a rule among yourselves that no excommunicated person shall be heard in a lay court; and I have seen by a letter sealed with thirty-two seals that you are excommunicated. Wherefore I shall not listen to you until such time as you are absolved."

I tell you this because through his own good sense alone he acquitted himself of what he had to do.

Abbot Geoffrey of St. Urban's, after I had gained his cause for him, returned me evil for good, and appealed against me. He gave our sainted king to understand that he was under his protection. I asked the king to ascertain the truth upon this point, whether the guardianship of the abbey rested with him or with me.

"Sire," said the abbot, "you shall not do that, please God; but keep us in your hands by commanding that the cause be pleaded between us and the Seigneur de Joinville; for we would rather that the abbey should be under your protection than under his to whom the heritage belongs."

Then the king said to me: "Is it true what they say, that the patronage of the abbey is mine?"

"Certes, sire," I replied, "it is not yours, but mine."

Thereupon the king answered: "It may well be that the heritage is yours, but still that you have no right to the guardianship of this abbey. But it is necessary, since you wish it," said he to the abbot, "and according to what you say and what the seneschal says, that it should remain either in his hands or in mine. I shall not fail, whatever you may say, to ascertain the truth ; for if I placed him under the necessity of pleading, I should do him a wrong, seeing that he is my vassal, in calling his title into court, which title he offers to prove to me satisfactorily."

He did ascertain the truth, and then consigned to me the guardianship of the abbey, and gave me letters from himself.

It came to pass that the sainted king exerted himself so much that the king of England, his wife, and children, came to France to treat with him about peace between him and them. Those of his council were strongly opposed to this peace, and said to him :—

" Sire, we greatly marvel that it should be your pleasure to yield to the King of England such a large portion of your land, which you and your predecessors have won from him, and through forfeiture. Wherefore it seems to us that if you believe you have no right to it, you do not make fitting restitution to the King of England unless you restore to him all the conquests which you and your predecessors have made ; but if you believe that you have a right to it, it seems to us that you are throwing away all that you yield to him."

To that the sainted king replied after this fashion :— " Sirs, I am certain that the King of England's predecessors lost most justly the conquests I hold ; and the land which I give up to him I do not give as a thing to which I am bound either towards himself or his heirs, but to create love between his children and mine, who are cousins-german. And it seems to me that I am making a good use of what I give to him, because he was not before my vassal, but now he has to render homage to me."

No man in the world ever worked harder to make peace between his subjects, especially between powerful neighbours and the princes of the realm, for example, between the Count of Châlons, uncle of the Seigneur de Joinville, and his son, the Count of Burgundy, who were at war with one another when we returned from beyond sea. To make peace between father and son, he sent his own counsellors into Burgundy, and at his own charges; and through his intervention peace was concluded between father and son. At a later period there was great contest between King Thibaud of Champagne, second of that name, and Count John of Châlons and the Count of Burgundy, his son, for the Abbey of Luxeuil. To allay this strife Monseigneur the King despatched Monseigneur Gervaise d'Escraines, who was at that time master-cook of France, and by his means he reconciled them.

After this dispute which the king terminated, there arose another great war between Count Thibaud of Bar and Count Henry of Luxemburg, whose wife was Thibaud's sister; and it thus chanced that they fought with one another near Pincy, and Count Thibaud of Bar took Count Henry of Luxemburg prisoner, and captured the castle of Linay, which belonged to the Count of Luxemburg by right of his wife. To appease this strife the king sent Monseigneur Peter the Chamberlain, the man in whom of all others he placed the most confidence, and this at the king's charges; and the king so exerted himself that they were reconciled.

With respect to these foreigners whom the king had reconciled, some of his council said that he did not act wisely in preventing them from warring upon one another; for if he let them impoverish themselves, they would not be so likely to attack him as if they were rich. To that the king made answer and said that they spoke not well :—

" For if the neighbouring princes observed that I suffered them to go to war, they would take counsel together and say, ' It is through maliciousness that the king
suffers us to go to war.' Then it would follow that out
of the hatred they would bear to me they would come
and attack me, and I might lose thereby, without taking
into account that I should earn God's enmity, who has
said, ' Blessed are the peacemakers.' "

And the consequence was that the Burgundians and
Lorrainers, whom he had pacified, loved and obeyed him
to such a degree, that I have seen them come and plead
before the king in their suits with one another, at the
king's courts at Reims, at Paris, and at Orleans.

The king so loved God and His sweet Mother, that
whomsoever he was able to convict of having uttered an
indecent word or vile oath touching God and His Mother he caused to be severely punished. For instance, I
saw a goldsmith at Cæsarea placed by his orders on a
ladder, in shirt and drawers, with a pig's entrails round
his neck, and in such quantity that they reached to his
nose. And I have heard that since our return from
beyond the sea he ordered a burgess of Paris to be
branded on the nose and under-lip for the same offence;
but I did not see that. And the sainted king said : " I
would consent to be marked with a hot iron, on condition
that all profane oaths were banished from my kingdom."

I was twenty-two years in his company without ever
having heard him swear by God, His Mother, or His
saints ; but when he wished to affirm anything, he would
say, " Truly, it was so," or " Truly, it shall be so."

Never did I hear him name the devil, except in some
book in which it was proper to name him, or in the life
of the saints to whom the book alluded. And it is a
great disgrace to the kingdom of France, and to the king

when he suffers it, that one can hardly speak without saying "The devil take it!" And it is a great sin of speech when one devotes to the devil a man or woman who are given to God from the moment they are baptized. In the Joinville household, whoso utters such a word receives a box on the ears or a slap on the face, and bad language is thus almost entirely suppressed.

He asked me if I washed the feet of the poor on Holy Thursday, and I answered, "No;" for it did not seem to me a right thing to do. He said that I ought not to hold the poor in scorn, for God had made them. "Would you then do unwillingly yourself what the King of England does, who washes the feet of lepers and kisses them?"

Before he lay down in his bed he had his children brought to him, and related to them the actions of good kings and emperors, and told them to take example by such men. And he likewise related to them the actions of bad princes, who, by their luxury, rapine, and avarice, had lost their kingdoms. "And I remind you of these things," said he, "that you may keep yourself from them, so that God be not angered against you." He made them learn their prayers to Our Lady, and made them repeat their Hours twice a day, to accustom them to hear their Hours when they should come to govern their lands.

The king was such a bountiful almoner that wherever he went through his kingdom, he made donations to poor churches, lazaretti, town-halls, hospitals, and men and women of gentle blood reduced to poverty. Every day he fed a multitude of poor people, without reckoning those who dined in his chamber; and many a time I have seen him cut bread for them and pour them out drink.

In his time were built several abbeys ; to wit, Royaumont, St. Antoine-lez-Paris, Lys, Maubuisson, and several other monasteries of Dominicans and Franciscans.
He built the Hôtel-Dieu at Pontoise and at Vernon, the
home for the blind at Paris, and the abbey of Franciscan sisters at St. Cloud, which his sister, Madame Isabelle, founded with his permission.

When any benefices of the holy Church lapsed to
him, before he bestowed them he consulted worthy persons, both those connected with religion and laics ; and
when he had taken counsel he bestowed these benefices
conscientiously, loyally, and according to God. He
would never give a benefice to any clerk until he had
renounced whatever other benefices he might possess.
In every town of his kingdom where he had never before
been, he went to the Dominicans and Franciscans, if
there were any, to obtain their prayers.

The provostship of Paris was at that time sold to the
burgesses of Paris or to others ; and when it happened
that some of them had purchased it, they countenanced
their sons and nephews in their misconduct ; for the
young people relied upon their parents and friends who
held the provostship. In consequence whereof the common people were much harassed, and could obtain no
justice against the rich by reason of the great presents
and gifts which these made to the provosts. In those
times whoso spoke the truth before the provost, or
wished to keep his oath so as not to perjure himself,
with regard to a debt or any other matter concerning
which he had to give witness, was subjected by the
provost to a fine and was punished. Because of the
gross injustice and robbery committed within the provostship, the common people were afraid to remain in
the king's land, but went to dwell in other provostships

and lordships. And the king's land was so deserted that, when he held his court of pleas, not more than ten or a dozen persons came to it. With that there were so many malefactors and thieves in Paris and the country around, that every place was full of them. The king, who was very anxious that the common people should be protected, learned the whole truth; and after that he would not suffer the provostship of Paris to be sold, but gave a large and handsome salary to those who were thenceforth to hold it. And he abolished all the harsh imposts by which the people were oppressed, and instituted search throughout the whole kingdom and country to find a man who would render strict and true justice, and would spare the rich man no more than the poor. There was pointed out to him Stephen Boileau, who so well maintained and looked after the provostship that no malefactor, thief, or murderer dared remain in Paris, for he was sure to be speedily hanged or otherwise executed; neither relationship, nor lineage, nor gold, nor silver could save him. The king's land soon improved; and people came there for the sake of the justice that was administered there. It then became peopled, and improved so much that sales, seizins, purchases, and other things were worth double what the king used previously to receive from them.

From his very childhood the king took pity on the poor and afflicted; and the custom was that, wherever the king went, a hundred and twenty poor persons should every day have an abundant meal in his house of bread, wine, and meat, or fish. In Lent and Advent the number of the poor was increased; and several times it happened that the king waited upon them and placed food before them, and carved for them, and gave them

money with his own hand when they went away. Parti-
cularly at the great vigils of solemn festivals he waited
upon the poor, as above related, before he himself eat
or drank anything. Besides all that, he had every day
to dine and sup with him old men and cripples, to whom
he gave of the same dishes that he himself partook of;
and when they had eaten they carried away a certain
sum in money. In addition to all that, the king bestowed every day such large and munificent donations
upon poor friars, poor hospitals, poor sick persons, poor
communities, poor gentlemen, poor dames and damsels
of gentle blood, upon women in reduced circumstances,
poor widows, women lying-in, and upon poor people
who, through sickness or old age, were unable to work
or follow their trade, that it is well nigh impossible to
reckon up the amount. So that we may say of him
that he was happier than Titus, Emperor of Rome, of
whom the ancient writers relate that he was greatly
afflicted and disconcerted when a day passed in which
he had not performed some good deed. From the time
he came to govern his realm and began to know himself,
he commenced building churches and religious houses,
among which the abbey of Royaumont excels all others
in beauty and grandeur. He erected several Hôtels-
Dieu, that of Paris, that of Pontoise, that of Compiègne,
that of Vernon, and conferred upon them much land.
He gave authority to his mother to found the abbey of
Lys, near Melun-sur-Seine, and that near Pontoise,
named Maubuisson. And he caused to be built the
Home for the Blind, near Paris, for the benefit of the
blind people of the city of Paris, and made them a
chapel wherein to hear God's worship. The good king
ordered the erection of the monastery of the Chartreux
without the walls of Paris, and assigned sufficient lands

P

to the monks who were there and served our Lord.
A short time afterwards he built another house without
the walls of Paris on the road to St. Denis, which was
called the Maison des Filles-Dieu, and placed in it a
great number of women who, through poverty, had
incurred the sin of wantonness, and gave them 400 *livres*
a-year for their support.   In several other parts of his
kingdom he built houses for nuns, and gave lands to
maintain them, and commanded them to receive such
women as were willing to pledge themselves to live
chastely.   Some of his intimates murmured at his
giving such large alms, and at his spending so much
money; and he replied, " I would rather that the
excess of the great expenditure I make should be
made in alms for the love of God than in pomp or vain
glory."

However, notwithstanding the great outlay he made
on alms, he did not for that omit to expend daily a large
sum of money in his palace. The king bore himself
liberally and generously in the parliaments and assem-
blies of the barons and knights; and the service of his
court was conducted very courteously, in a very open-
handed manner, and without stint, far more so than had
been the case for a long time at the courts of his predecessors.

After the things above related it came to pass that
the king summoned all his barons to Paris at the sea-
son of Lent (A. D. 1267). I excused myself on account
of a quartan fever which I had at the time, and begged
him to dispense with my attendance. But he sent me
word that he insisted upon my going, for he had skilful
physicians who were able to cure the quartan fever.
So I went to Paris. When I arrived, on the vigil of
Our Lady in March, I found neither the king nor any

one who could tell me why the king had summoned me.
And it happened, as God willed, that I fell asleep during
matins, and while I slept it seemed to me that I beheld
the king before an altar upon his knees, and methought
I saw many prelates in full canonicals put on him a red
chasuble of Reims serge. After this vision I called to
me Monseigneur William, my priest, a man of much
knowledge, and related it to him. And he replied : " Sir,
you will see that the king will take the cross to-morrow."
I asked him why he thought so ; and he answered that
he thought so because of the dream I had had ; for the
chasuble of red serge signified the cross, which was red
with the blood that God had shed from His side, and
hands, and feet. " As for the chasuble being of Reims
serge, that signifies that the crusade will be of little
profit, as you will see if God give you life."

When I had heard mass at the Magdalen at Paris I
went to the king's chapel, and found him mounted upon
the platform where the relics were, and bringing down
the true cross. While the king was coming down, two
knights who were of his council began to speak to one
another, and one of them said :—

" Never believe me, if the king is not going to take
the cross."

Whereupon the other replied : " If the king takes the
cross, it will be one of the saddest days that ever befell
France. For if we do not take the cross, we shall lose
the king's affection ; and if we do take the cross,
we shall lose God's favour, because it will not be on His
account that we shall take it."

And it came to pass that on the morrow the king took
the cross, and his three sons with him ; and afterwards
it proved that the crusade was of little profit, according
to my priest's prophecy. I was much pressed by the

King of France and the King of Navarre to take the
cross, whereto I replied that while I was serving God
and the king beyond sea, and since my return, the sergeants of the King of France and of the King of Navarre had ruined myself and impoverished my people,
so that no time could ever come when they and I should
be worse off than we were; and I also told them that if
I wished to do what was pleasing unto God, I should
remain here to aid and defend my people, for if I risked
my person in the adventures of the pilgrimage of the
cross, where I saw clearly that it would be for the hurt
and damage of my people, I should bring down upon
myself the wrath of God, who gave up His life to save
His people.

I considered that all those committed a deadly sin
who advised him to that voyage, because France was in
that state that the entire kingdom was at peace within
itself and with all its neighbours; and after he departed
its condition has never ceased to grow worse and worse.
They committed a great sin who counselled him that
voyage, in the great weakness to which his body was reduced, for he was unable to go either in a carriage or on
horseback. His weakness was so great that he allowed
me to carry him in my arms from the house of the
Count of Auxerre, where I took leave of him, to the
Franciscans. And yet, weak as he was, had he remained
in France, he might have lived for many a year and
done much good.

Of the voyage he made to Tunis I do not mean to
relate or say anything, because, thank God, I was not
there; and I do not wish to say anything or put
anything in my book of which I am not certain.
We will speak, then, of our sainted king without
more ado, and will say that after he had landed at Tunis,

before the Castle of Carthage, he was seized with
dysentery, for which he took to bed, and was sensible
that he must soon pass from this world to the next.
Thereupon he called Monseigneur Philip, his son,
and commanded him to observe, as if it were a will,
all the instructions he left him, which instructions
the king, it is said, wrote out with his own sainted
hand.

"Fair son, the first thing I teach thee is to mould thy
heart to love God; for without that no one can be saved.
Take care not to do anything which may displease
God, to wit, a deadly sin ; on the contrary, thou shouldst
endure all sorts of outrage and torture rather than commit a deadly sin. If God send thee adversity, accept it
patiently, and render thanks to our Lord, and think that
thou hast deserved it, and that it will turn wholly to
thy advantage. If He bestows upon thee prosperity,
thank Him humbly, so that thou art not worse through
pride or other cause when thou oughtest to be better ;
for no one ought to war against God with gifts. Confess
thyself frequently, and choose as confessor a man of dis-
cretion, who shall teach thee what thou oughtest to do
and what thou oughtest to avoid. And thou shouldst
bear and comport thyself in such manner that thy confessor and friends may venture to reprove thee for thy
misdeeds. Attend devoutly to the service of the Holy
Church, both with heart and mouth, especially at mass
during the consecration. Let thy heart be gentle
and compassionate towards the poor, the unfortunate,
and the afflicted, and comfort and help them so far as
in thee lies. Maintain the good customs of thy kingdom, and put down the bad. Be not covetous against
thy people, and do not load thy conscience with imposts
and taxes. If thou hast any sorrow at heart, tell it

straightway to thy confessor, or to some discreet man who is not full of idle words; then thou wilt bear it more easily. Take care to have in thy company discreet and loyal persons, whether religious or secular, who are not full of covetousness, and converse frequently with them; but flee and avoid the society of the wicked. Listen gladly to the word of God, and keep it in thy heart; and seek earnestly for prayers and indulgences. Love what is good and profitable; hate whatever is evil, wherever it be. Let no one be so bold as to utter before thee any word that may lead to or excite a sin, or to speak evil of others behind their backs; neither suffer any profane thing to be said of God in thy presence. Render thanks frequently to God for all the good things He has bestowed upon thee, so that thou be worthy of still greater blessings. In administering justice and doing right to thy subjects be loyal and firm, without turning to the right hand or to the left; but help the right, and uphold the complaint of the poor man until the truth be made manifest. And if any one has an action against thee, do not believe anything until thou knowest the whole truth; for then thy counsellors will judge more boldly according to truth, either for or against thee. If thou hast anything that belongeth to another, either through thee or thy predecessors, and the thing be certain, make restitution without delay; but if the thing be doubtful, institute an inquiry into it by means of wise men, promptly and diligently. It is thy duty to take care that thy people and subjects live under thee in peace and uprightness. Above all, keep the good towns and customs of thy kingdom in the condition and liberties in which thy predecessors preserved them; and if there be anything to amend, amend and redress it, and keep them in favour and affection; for because of

the power and riches of the great cities thy subjects and
foreigners will fear to do anything against thee, especially thy peers and thy barons. Honour and love all
persons belonging to the Holy Church, and take heed
that no one wrests from them, or diminishes the gifts
and alms which thy predecessors have bestowed. It is
related of King Philip, my grandfather, that on one
occasion one of his counsellors told him that the people
of the Holy Church did him much wrong in that they
infringed his rights and encroached upon his jurisdic-
tion, and that it was great marvel he suffered it; and
the good king answered, that he was well aware of it;
but when he reflected upon the goodness and favour
God had shown to himself, he preferred to lose something of his rights than to have any dispute with the
people of the Holy Church. To thy father and thy
mother show honour and respect, and keep their commandments. Bestow the benefices of the Holy Church
upon persons of worth and of unspotted lives; and act
by the advice of wise and honourable men. Take care
not to undertake a war against a Christian prince without grave deliberation; and if it be necessary for thee
to do so, watch over the Holy Church and those who
have done thee no wrong. If wars and disputes arise
between thy subjects, appease them as speedily as thou
canst. Be careful to have good provosts and bailiffs,
and make frequent inquiries about them and the people
of thy household, as to how they conduct themselves,
and if they are guilty of over-much greed, or of treach-
ery or deceit. Labour to root out of thy kingdom all
vile sinfulness; especially put down with all thy might
profane oaths and heresy. Take heed that the charges
of thy household be reasonable. Lastly, sweet son,
cause masses to be chanted and prayers offered up for

my soul throughout thy kingdom; and grant me a spe-
cial and positive part in all the good that thou shalt do.
Fair dear son, I bestow upon thee all the benedictions
that a good father can give unto a son. And may the
blessed Trinity preserve and defend thee from all evil;
and may God give thee grace, to do always His will, so
that He may be honoured by thee, and that thou and I,
after this mortal life, may be together with Him, and
praise Him without end. Amen."

When the good king had given his instructions to his
son, Monseigneur Philip, the sickness that was upon him
began to increase greatly; whereupon he asked for the
sacraments of the holy church, and received them with
sound understanding and in full consciousness, as appeared by this, that while they were anointing him with
holy oil, and saying the seven psalms, he repeated the
verses in his turn. And I have heard it stated by Monseigneur the Count of Alençon, his son, that when death
was at hand, he called upon the saints to aid and succour him, and especially upon Monseigneur St. James,
repeating his collect which begins with *Esto, Domine*,
that is, " O God, be Thou the sanctifier and guardian of
Thy people." He then called to his aid Monseigneur
St. Denis of France, repeating his collect which signifies, " Sire God, grant unto us that we may despise the
prosperity of this world, so that we may not fear any
adversity."

And I have heard Monseigneur d'Alençon say that
his father next invoked St. Geneviève. After that, the
sainted king caused himself to be laid on a bed covered
with ashes, and placed his hands upon his breast, and,
looking up to heaven, yielded up his spirit to our Creator,
at the very same hour that the Son of God died upon
the cross.

It is a precious and worthy act to mourn the death of this sainted prince who governed his kingdom so devoutly and loyally, bestowed so many and such liberal alms, and established in it so many fine institutions. In like manner, as a writer who has finished his book illuminates it with gold and azure, so did the king illuminate his kingdom with the fine abbeys he built in it, Hôtels-Dieu, and convents of Dominicans, Franciscans, and other religious orders above-named.

On the day after the festival of St. Bartholomew the Apostle, passed from this world the good King Louis, in the year of our Lord's incarnation, and in the year of grace 1270; and his bones were preserved in a coffer, and buried at St. Denis in France, which he had selected for his place of burial; and at the spot where he was interred God has wrought many a fine miracle for the sake of his deserts.

At a later period, on the requisition of the King of France, and, by the Pope's command, the Archbishop of Rouen and brother John of Samois, who was afterwards a bishop, came to St. Denis in France, where they tarried a long time to prosecute the inquiry into the life, works, and miracles of the sainted king. I was summoned to go to them, and they detained me two days. And after they had made inquisition of myself and others, what they had learnt was carried to the Court of Rome; and the pope and the cardinals carefully examined what was brought to them; and as they saw fit they did him justice, and placed him in the number of martyr-confessors. Whence there was, and well might be, great rejoicing throughout the entire kingdom of France, and great honour to all those of his lineage who would resemble him in doing good. Yes, great honour to all those of his lineage who by their works shall seek to imitate him; but great dishonour to those of his lineage who shall elect to do evil, for people will point the finger at them, and will say that the sainted king from whom they are descended would never have consented to do such an evil action.

After these good tidings had been received from Rome, the king appointed the day after the feast of St. Bartholomew (August 25th, A.D. 1298), and on that day the sanctified body was taken up. When it was lifted out of the ground, the archbishop of Reims of that time (whom may God absolve!), and Monseigneur Henry de Villers, my nephew, who was then Archbishop of Lyons, carried it forward, as did many other archbishops and bishops whom I cannot now name. It was borne to a raised platform erected for the purpose.

Brother John of Samois preached on that occasion; and among other great actions which our sainted king had performed, he mentioned some of those to which I had testified on oath, and which I had myself witnessed. "That you may see that he was the most loyal man of his time, I will tell you that he was so loyal that he insisted upon fulfilling, in the case even of Saracens, a promise he had made to them upon his simple word, and had he not kept faith with them, he would have gained 10,000 *livres* and more." And he related to them the incident as it has been here written down.

And when he had recounted the circumstances, he said, "Do not fancy that I am lying to you, for I see a man here who has testified to this matter upon oath."

When the sermon was finished, the king and his brothers carried back the sanctified body into the Church, with the aid of such of their lineage as were entitled to that honour, for a great honour has been

conferred upon them, if they do not themselves place
any obstacle in the way, as I have already remarked.
Let us beseech him to pray unto God to give us what is
needful for our souls and bodies.   Amen.

I wish to tell you yet of our sainted king things that
are to his honour, to wit, that it seemed to me in a dream,
that I beheld him in front of my chapel at Joinville,
and methought he was marvellously cheerful and light-
hearted; and I also was very happy at seeing him in
my castle, and I said to him, " Sire, when you depart
from here, I will lodge you in a house of mine that is
in one of my towns named Chevillon."   And he
answered me with a laugh and said: " Sire de Joinville, by the faith which I owe you, I have no desire to
depart so soon from here."

When I awoke, I reflected upon this, and it seemed
to me that it pleased God and himself that I should
lodge him in my chapel, and I did so, for I erected an
altar in honour of God, and of himself, and there is
land in perpetuity settled for this purpose.   These
matters I have related to Monseigneur King Louis, who
is heir to his name, and it seems to me that he would
do what would be pleasing unto God and to our
sainted King Louis, if he were to procure relics of the
true sanctified body, and send them to the said chapel
of St. Laurent at Joinville, so that those who approach
his altar may do so with the greater devotion.

I make known unto all that I have put down here
a great number of the actions of our sainted king
above named, which I witnessed and heard, and also a
great number which I have found in a history written
in French, which I have caused to be transcribed into
this book.   And I mention this, that whoso shall hear

this book read aloud, may believe firmly what the book says, which I have verily seen and heard.

This was written in the year of grace 1309, in the month of October.

THE END.

CHISWICK PRESS :—PRINTED BY WHITTINGHAM AND WILKINS, TOOKS COURT, CHANCERY LANE.

The Bayard Series.

COMPRISING

PLEASURE BOOKS OF LITERATURE PRODUCED IN THE CHOICEST STYLE, AS COMPANIONABLE VOLUMES AT HOME AND ABROAD.

Price 2s. 6d. each Vol., complete in itself, printed at the Chiswick Press, bound by Burn, flexible cloth extra, gilt leaves, with silk Headbands and Registers.

SOCRATES (MEMOIRS OF). By EDWARD LEVIEN, M.A.

MY UNCLE TOBY: His Story and His Friends. Edited by P. FITZGERALD.

REFLECTIONS; or, Moral Sentences and Maxims of the Duke de la Rochefoucauld.

ESSAYS IN MOSAIC.

THE STORY OF THE CHEVALIER BAYARD. By M. DE BERVILLE.

DE JOINVILLE'S ST LOUIS, KING OF FRANCE.

THE ESSAYS OF ABRAHAM COWLEY, including all his Prose Works.

ABDALLAH; OR, THE FOUR LEAVES. By EDOUARD LABOULLAYE.

TABLE-TALK AND OPINIONS OF NAPOLEON BUONAPARTE.

VATHEK: AN ORIENTAL ROMANCE. By WILLIAM BECKFORD.

THE KING AND THE COMMONS: A Selection of Cavalier and Puritan Song. Edited by Professor MORLEY.

WORDS OF WELLINGTON: Maxims and Opinions of the Great Duke.

DR JOHNSON'S RASSELAS, PRINCE OF ABYSSINIA. With Notes.

HAZLITT'S ROUND TABLE. With Biographical Introduction.

THE RELIGIO MEDICI, HYDRIOTAPHIA, AND THE LETTER TO A FRIEND. By Sir THOMAS BROWNE, Knt.

BALLAD POETRY OF THE AFFECTIONS. By ROBERT BUCHANAN.

COLERIDGE'S CHRISTABEL, and other Imaginative Poems. With Preface by ALGERNON C. SWINBURNE.

LORD CHESTERFIELD'S LETTERS, SENTENCES, AND MAXIMS. With Introduction by the Editor, and Essay on Chesterfield by M. DE ST BEUVE, of the French Academy.

Other Volumes in Active Progress.

A suitable Case containing 12 volumes, price 31s. 6d.; or the Case separate, price 3s. 6d.

EXTRACTS FROM LITERARY NOTICES.

"The present series—taking its name from the opening volume, which contained a translation of the Knight without Fear and without Reproach—will really, we think, fill a void in the shelves of all except the most complete English libraries. These little square-shaped volumes contain, in a very manageable and pretty form, a great many things not very easy of access elsewhere, and some things for the first time brought together."—*Pall Mall Gazette.* "We have here two more volumes of the series appropriately called the 'Bayard,' as they certainly are *sans reproche.* Of convenient size, with clear typography and tasteful binding, we know no other little volumes which make such good giftbooks for persons of mature age."—*Examiner.* "St Louis and his companions, as described by Joinville, not only in their glistening armour, but in their everyday attire, are brought nearer to us, become intelligible to us, and teach us lessons of humanity which we can learn from men only, and not from saints and heroes. Here lies the real value of real history. It widens our minds and our hearts, and gives us that true knowledge of the world and of human nature in all its phases which but few can gain in the short span of their own life, and in the narrow sphere of their friends and enemies. We can hardly imagine a better book for boys to read or for men to ponder over."—*Times.* "Every one of the works included in this series is well worth possessing, and the whole will make an admirable foundation for the library of a studious youth of polished and refined tastes."—*Illustrated Times.*

The Gentle Life Series.

Printed in Elzevir, on Toned Paper, handsomely bound, forming suitable Volumes for Presents.

Price 6s. each; or in calf extra, price 10s. 6d.

I.

THE GENTLE LIFE. Essays in Aid of the Formation of Character of Gentlemen and Gentlewomen. Tenth Edition.

"His notion of a gentleman is of the noblest and truest order. The volume is a capital specimen of what may be done by honest reason, high feeling, and cultivated intellect. A little compendium of cheerful philosophy."—*Daily News.*

"Deserves to be printed in letters of gold, and circulated in every house."—*Chambers' Journal.*

II.

ABOUT IN THE WORLD. Essays by the Author of "The Gentle Life."

"It is not easy to open it at any page without finding some happy idea."—*Morning Post.*

III.

LIKE UNTO CHRIST. A new Translation of the "De Imitatione Christi," usually ascribed to THOMAS À KEMPIS. With a Vignette from an Original Drawing by Sir THOMAS LAWRENCE. Second Edition.

"Evinces independent scholarship, a profound feeling for the original, and a minute attention to delicate shades of expression, which may well make it acceptable even to those who can enjoy the work without a translator's aid."—*Nonconformist.*

"Could not be presented in a more exquisite form, for a more sightly volume was never seen."—*Illustrated London News.*

IV.

FAMILIAR WORDS. An Index Verborum, or Quotation Handbook. Affording an immediate Reference to Phrases and Sentences that have become imbedded in the English Language. Second and enlarged Edition.

"Should be on every library table, by the side of Roget's 'Thesaurus.'"—*Daily News.*

V.

ESSAYS BY MONTAIGNE. Edited, Compared, Revised, and Annotated by the Author of "The Gentle Life." With Vignette Portrait. Second Edition.

"We should be glad if any words of ours could help to bespeak a large circulation for this handsome attractive book; and who can refuse his homage to the good-humoured industry of the editor."—*Illustrated Times.*

VI.

THE COUNTESS OF PEMBROKE'S ARCADIA. Written by Sir PHILIP SYDNEY. Edited, with Notes, by the Author of "The Gentle Life." Dedicated, by permission, to the Earl of Derby. 7s. 6d.

"All the best things in the Arcadia are retained intact in Mr Friswell's edition, and even brought into greater prominence than in the original, by the curtailment of some of its inferior portions, and the omission of most of its eclogues and other metrical digressions."—*Examiner.*